Goose River Anthology, 2013

Edited by

Deborah J. Benner

Goose River Press
Waldoboro, Maine

Published by
Goose River Press
3400 Friendship Road
Waldoboro ME 04572
gooseriverpress@roadrunner.com
www.gooseriverpress.com

Goose River Anthology, 2013//ii

Table of Contents

Table of Contents

Table of Contents

Table of Contents

Table of Contents

Dedicated to our beautiful new
daughter-in-law, Eva.

Welcome to the family, honey.

T. Blen Parker
Richmond, ME

Life on Swango

Both grandparents had very strong Maine accents, not uncommon for their generation, but the way they spoke was a source of embarrassment to me. Around the time I started first grade I had my first teacher-parent consult inside the school and Gramie came into the classroom to collect me early. It was at that time I realized not everyone lived with grandparents, what old fashioned meant and that not everyone understood why I lived with them on that State Game Preserve island. What embarrassed me then only warms my heart now. To hear one more *by gorry* now would be music to my ears. Listening to hours of seamstress tips or dress-designing instructions would put a smile on my face from ear to ear. Seeing her walk into a room with her silvery braid, I would run to her with open arms. I wouldn't be able to resist snapping his suspenders, just a little.

Starting with her sensible black leather shoes, always laced, ending in a bow above her ankle, I saw her crisply ironed, cotton housedress with the long sleeves rolled up to her elbows. Covering most of the dress was usually an over-the-head full apron in a cotton print, tied in a crisscross across her shoulders ending in a bow at her waist. Sometimes on special occasions she would wear her more formal half aprons, like for Thanksgiving dinners. The shoes came from Sears by catalog order but the dresses and house-dresses were handmade on her treadle sewing machine, carefully and with love.

She was most happy whenever she was sewing, singing hymns in a low voice or whistling to herself as she went along the seams, being ever so mindful of her stitch length as she pedaled. I loved to sit quietly and watch her from the floor behind the sewing machine bench. Her silvery hair was waist length. Each day she would brush and comb it before braid-

T. Blen Parker
Richmond, ME

ing it into one long, single braid that she pinned with tiny hairpins into a beautiful halo around her head. The braiding was part of her early morning routine. She let me watch her brush, brush, and braid that beautiful hair. She was such a goddess to me.

"For heavens sake," she burst out suddenly. "You'd think it was his buuthdee er somethin," with the hint of a scowl on her pretty face. She had asked him what he would like for supper that night. Before making the trip overstreet from island to mainland, she wanted to insure he had a list to take up to Rink's Market on the corner of Main and Front Streets in downtown Richmond. She asked him to bring some cottage cheese, knowing it was something she could always get me to eat.

"By gorry, I think mebbe onions, those little white ones you boil up, some-ah-those baby peas and a good hunk a steak sounds good, since ya asked," he smiled across the kitchen at her. He added, "Some-a-that stinky-feet cheese to go on the side ah my plate too." He was referring to pearl onions, the cube steak she regularly fried to death in the big black cast iron spider and a wedge of strong cheese cut from the big cheese round at the local market.

I never could figure out how he could eat steak *with no teeth,* but he loved it. He had nothing good to say about false teeth, glasses or hearing aids. I couldn't imagine him with any of those things, but it isn't like his life wouldn't have been better for using them. I knew no other Grampie, just became accustomed to him that way. He was a magician—a hero to me. I watched, clapping each time he could successfully line up ten baby peas on a butter knife and all at once slip them into his mouth without dropping even one. Gramie looked on with her head half lowered, pretending my delighted giggling wasn't happening at all. Her effort to be stern enough to teach me table manners was highly unsuccessful during those particular meals. She couldn't hide her smirk. It was a loving moment I will long remember.

T. Blen Parker
Richmond, ME

They shared a warm smile, a kiss and he was on his way in the truck, down to the dock where he would maneuver the flat bottomed, flat bow metal boat he named *Swanee* across the river to the Richmond dock to tie up. He'd walk uptown to do his shopping in better weather, sometimes driving the old beater-car he had parked in the lot there at the landing if it was raining or snowing, providing the gasoline had not been siphoned off by some of the less than reputable local boys.

Her instructions while he was gone, "Mind ya, I'll only be a minute, gotta go down to the 'roet cella' to fetch some taatahs for suppah. You can sott out all the *red* buttons while I'm down theah." I begin by dumping the gallon-sized pickle jar full of old buttons onto the worn Persian rug. She saved buttons from worn out clothing, often buying sale bin buttons just to have them in a pinch. She bought many when they were ten cents for six on a card at Woolworth's, Reny's or at the Five and Dime in Gardiner. She returned with the potatoes and some fresh peas from the garden, wrapped in the front of her apron like a package held before her. Her aprons served multi-purposes. They covered her pretty housedresses, could serve as tote bags for garden vegetables, wipe tears from a skinned knee victim or dried hands when no towel was near. At times, the folded over corner of an apron might serve as a hot pad in a pinch. One never knew when the lid of that old stained bean pot might need to be lifted just to stir in the salt pork. Much to her surprise, I had artistically assembled the letters of the alphabet from A–G in buttons upon her return. She was as totally amazed as I was to have done the letters correctly.

She began to peel the potatoes preparing them to boil in a pan of lightly salted water on the wood stovetop. The peelings went into a swill bucket for the deer, kept out on the piazza for Grampie to take on his trip down the island road to mix in with the grain in a trough as their supper. He would drive in first gear all the way to the end of the island road,

T. Blen Parker
Richmond, ME

sometimes stopping completely to call out the open driver's window, "Baby, ohhh Bayyyy-bbbeeee." Most of the time at least one or two does would saunter out of the woods, knowing there was a special treat that night. He would let me gently hand out pieces of stale bread for the bravest ones who dared to approach the truck with the engine still running.

Gramie was adept in her kitchen and pantry. Gathering as many things as could fit into the front fold of her apron, she prepared to make her wonderful, light-as-a-feather biscuits. Out came the big, heavy, wooden flour board. She would first sprinkle a *scarce amount* as she explained, of flour down on the board when cutting out cookies, rolling out piecrusts or cutting biscuits. Next she retrieved the Morton's salt with the pinafore girl walking in the rain, the Clabber girl baking powder, the flour canister, (a three-gallon tin which formerly served as a Humpty Dumpty potato chip can). The tin measuring cup followed, a set of tin measuring spoons, the oversized tin biscuit cutter with the green wooden handle, a long handled wooden spoon and her last item, a large and heavy crackled finish yellow pottery mixing bowl.

Gramie had staged her work area. That was my cue to search for the turtle stool that Grampie had made me for observing from just the right height at the table. He had painted the stool green with black turtle features, eyes, toenails and shell. I could stand or sit on it whichever worked best depending on the activity. It was one of the things I treasured as all mine.

Just then we both turned to see him return from *overstreet* in his baggy, olive workpants held up by wide, red suspenders slid over his olive work shirt. On the left shoulder rode the State of Maine Game Warden patch that Gramie had so carefully sewn on with her treadle sewing machine. He was holding four of the first recyclable bags styles that Gramie had made out of flour sacks with two cloth handles. They were sturdy tote bags, perfect for river crossings. "Gotta go fill that generatah again, forgoht to do it this foahnoon.

T. Blen Parker
Richmond, ME

There'll be no news tonight fi don't." He continued tromping through the kitchen as a shortcut to the woodshed, chawing on his wad of chewing tobaccy.

He was referring to the only source of electricity for the house, a noisy and unreliable gas generator used sparingly to watch TV, local news and maybe *Beat the Clock, Ed Sullivan Show, What's My Line* or *Perry Como Show* each night after supper. She just smiled, continuing to make her heavenly biscuits as I watched on contentedly. Chalk this one up as just another day in the life on the Steve Powell, Wildlife Management Island residents during the 1950's in Maine.

***

Janet Leahy
New Berlin, WI

One with Weather

Rain rains making the garden glad.
Snow snows in a flurry of white.
Hail hails us to the window.
Sleet sleets across the yard.
Wind winds through the pine, calling our name.
Clouds cloud our vision, we question what it is we know.
Humidity hangs humid drops of moisture close around us.
Fog, in a foggy scrim, erases our world.
Storms storm through our lives.
Lightning lights the night, violent and electric.
Thunder thunders across the sky, no one, not even the dog
       sleeps.
We weather the weather, season after season.

Earl Weigelt
Winslow, ME

Clumps of Fleece

Sheep like their paths well-worn and easy,
fit for woolly followership.
They're fond from muddy puddles to drink
though streams nearby run clearly.
And sheep love to bunt and kick,
all stubborn and resolute—
blinking, bleating, uncomprehending
while doom lurks grimly in the dark.

(All-for-one and One-for-all;
What's-mine-is-yours,
What's-yours-is-mine
Until you graze MY grass...)
And... if I simply hide my eyes
from the weather or the Wolf,
then by my will and ignorance
I'll thrust all threats aside.
Who needs the Shepherd with His crook?
Look, the pasture's clear!
And green's the forage, wide and near
as always it has been...
Why the Sheepdogs, those rangy mutts
scary, smelly, so uncouth;
watching, pacing, nosing breezes
...and looking like the Wolf?
And let the lambs just roam and skip
for don't they look so precious?
Never butt nor make them mind
nor acknowledge any fences.
(All-for-one and One-for-all;
What's-mine-is-yours,
What's-yours-is-mine
Until you graze MY grass...)

Liz Moser
Baltimore, MD and Phippsburg, ME

Rediscovered, Reinvented

Afterwards
from being told I carried a malignancy
that could already have attacked me fatally

I am suddenly reduced to the sum of my parts,
no more adventuring,
expansions into other ways and places.
I must consolidate, pick up my pieces, make order out of
scattered papers, empty files and
outworn shoes and sweaters.
My calendar is full of dates and question marks I will erase,
call off,
decide who needs to know I'm unavailable
indefinitely. I fade....

afterwards
when doctors' scalpels cut away the tumor,
leaving no disease
to feed the cancer, told me go about your life

I wake up drained and grateful,
mystified at why I have persistence and desire
to breathe, smile, interact again.

My gray boat passed
through unfamiliar tides and currents,
now is slid to shore. I am a shadow,
numb, unfeeling
till I absorb what once
was everyday with deepened breath.

Sally Belenardo
Branford, CT

Now I Lay Me Down to Sleep

Magnolias by the stone veranda
sweetened with every breath
springtimes lasting long as years
when trees all lived forever. Maples
guarded eaves and gables, shaded
garret windows, where I wondered if God
knew the sum of their leaves. Hemlocks
towered over the sun, holding
lavender clouds of dying days
as Gramma climbed the hallway stairs
to guide my way through rhyming prayers,
when life went on forever, one eve to wait
for footsteps and her voice no more—
same summer the hurricane would take
our graceful elms and lay them down
across the lawn, leaving a space
that brought to light the meaning
and the terror of
...If I should die before I wake...

John T. Hagan
Springboro, OH

Ties That Inspire

As my lovely date and I sat in the audience of Boardwalk Hall in Atlantic City on that warm September evening, I was struck by the substantial difference in the responses of the first four contestants from that of the fifth and last. Master of Ceremonies, Bert Parks, had asked each of the five finalists for the crown of Miss America what person had been most inspirational in her life and for what reasons. Given the pageant year's relative proximity to three national luminaries' untimely and violent deaths, they were aptly and predictably cited by three of the finalists as being profoundly influential. Miss Maine spoke of John F. Kennedy and his spirit of national service and optimism. Miss Colorado delineated the inspiration she derived from Martin Luther King's indefatigable pursuit of his dream for black America. Miss Wisconsin practically wept as she described the strength she drew from the zest for life and zeal for justice that abounded in Robert F. Kennedy. Drawing upon a more historic and international figure, Miss Ohio found motivation in the courage and resolve of Joan of Arc, and the Buckeye beauty deftly supported her choice of the French heroine with a quote from Mark Twain: "She is easily and by far the most extraordinary person the human race has ever produced."[*] When the fifth finalist, Miss Kentucky, cited her choice for an abidingly influential person, the nearly palpable shock that rippled across the large audience practically shouted that she had made a careless personal choice.

"For me," said Mary Beth Adkins, "Miss Hessie Pennix stands as the most admirable and humane person I know, and without her I would not be standing here tonight."

The crowd, of course, had no idea who Hessie Pennix was and likely wondered if Miss Kentucky had decided to throw in the towel by naming such an obscure personality, but I

John T. Hagan
Springboro, OH

knew the reasons for Mary Beth's thoughtful albeit risky selection. Miss Hester Pennix was a living legend in the area around the tiny town of Fisty in the Appalachian Mountain region of Knott County, Kentucky.

Miss Hessie, as she was affectionately known, was a graduate of Centre College in Danville, Kentucky, and she had emigrated after graduation from her home in Louisville to the mountains of Knott County. Fresh from college with a teaching certificate, she had responded to an announcement sent to Centre, stating the need for "a modestly paid 1-12 teacher for the children in the area of Fisty, Kentucky." The actual remuneration for the position made "modestly paid" one of the most colossal hyperboles in the history of recruiting legerdemain.

Hester Elinore Pennix moved into a second-floor bedroom of a boarding house in Fisty in August of 1922. Born the fourth child into a family of eight children in Louisville in 1901, her father was a mathematics professor at the University of Louisville, and her mother was a full-time parent and part-time seamstress. Uncommonly bright and unusually tall, the svelte and auburn-haired Hester had won a full scholarship to the prestigious Centre College at seventeen, and most of her instructors and classmates at the college assumed that when she graduated with a dual major in mathematics and English, she would accept the fellowship extended to her for master's work at Harvard University.

Miss Kentucky used her brief response time to provide the general reasons for her choice of Hessie Pennix: kindness, tenacity, generosity, altruism, and pedagogy. Naturally, Miss Kentucky's time limits restricted any expansion upon the contributions to Fisty, Kentucky that made Miss Hessie so noteworthy, but those who came of age near that eastern Kentucky town knew them well.

I was a skinny six-year-old when I joined the other students in the one-room schoolhouse situated near old-growth woods and reached by a sparsely graveled road that ran east

John T. Hagan
Springboro, OH

and west out of Fisty. I had three other "classmates," two boys and a girl, and our arrival that September for first grade augmented the aggregate school population to 39 pupils, ranging from grades one through twelve. I had already heard plenty about Miss Hessie from my three older brothers, one of whom was in the eighth grade and one in the ninth. My oldest brother, Randy, had dropped out after tenth grade to join my dad in a nearby coalmine.

Miss Hessie was well into her long career by the time I showed up with my lunch pail and book bag, and she bore a reputation as both a tough taskmaster and a consummate humanitarian. That reputation was not built upon hearsay.

The Great Depression that ravaged the nation through the thirties and early forties was especially hard on those around Fisty who knew stark privation as a way of life. Hessie's meager salary would fluctuate according to the economic times, but being the resourceful teacher she was, she not only made do with what she had but managed to provide assistance to a number of her destitute students. In the late nineteen-twenties she purchased a dilapidated bungalow at the edge of town, and with her own elbow grease and the assistance of townspeople, she was able to reconstitute the house into a charming refuge for her evenings of reading and baking. During the school months, Hessie would often bake biscuits during the nights before class days and bring them and a jar of honey to school for the children who often went without breakfast. Hessie made herself available to the families around Fisty in many ways, including visiting the sick, helping in the fields, and volunteering with the Red Cross. Quite attractive in her younger years, she had a number of suitors, but no relationship reached an engagement or marriage, and when questioned about having her own children, her standard reply was that she had a schoolroom full of them.

To me Miss Hessie gave no quarter, and from me she accepted no lame excuses for incomplete homework or slip-

John T. Hagan
Springboro, OH

shod class work. She obviously saw something in me I would likely have never seen in myself, and as I progressed through the grades, she relentlessly imposed more and more exasperating and sophisticated writing assignments upon me. I often bridled at her expectations, noting that my composition topics were more complex than those she gave pupils two or three years my senior. As I advanced in my education, I began to suspect some method to her madness, and while I never relished her challenges, I resolved to beat her at her own game. I began to accept her assignments as gauntlets I'd take up to make her cease and desist in my weekly torments. I was, however, the victim of my own successes, as they only increased the difficulty of my assignments.

The dictionary she lent me became my six-gun in our little duel, and although she frequently noted my "bigworditis," she seemed to applaud my efforts to expand my compositional horizons. By eleventh grade I was actually attempting some short stories and essays on my own, and I would proffer them for her perusal. Never the gusher, her slightest affirmation was grist for my further attempts, and by the beginning of my twelfth grade, she had me dreaming of college as an English or journalism major. Assisting me in my application, Miss Hessie's recommendation letter resulted in my admission to Vanderbilt University, and her cosigning of loans from the local bank helped to meet tuition expenses. I am now a syndicated writer, living in New York City. Were it not for Miss Hessie, I would likely be working today in the coalmines with my three brothers where my father contracted his fatal pneumoconiosis or black lung disease.

As I began my eighth year of studies, five first-graders entered our school, and of the two little boys and three little girls, a towheaded darling with a recently lost first tooth was among them. Her name was Mary Beth Adkins, and notwithstanding my indifference to the younger children, I took note of Miss Hessie's extraordinary attentions to her. Indeed, Mary Beth was a charmer although retiring and reticent.

John T. Hagan
Springboro, OH

Keeping daily tabs on Miss Hessie's efforts with Mary Beth, I couldn't help making comparisons to the demands upon the new student's development that were much the same as those she made upon me. Progressing through my high school studies, I became increasingly intrigued by the alacrity with which Mary Beth mastered her studies and the ease with which she emerged from her retiring persona.

Graduation, of course, took me to college in Nashville, Tennessee. My classes there as a duel major in English and journalism were most demanding and often frustrating. I was not only cast into a pool of competitors that included the most elite young scholars in the country, but my empirical knowledge of the world had been severely limited by my Appalachian origins. In fact, my classroom contributions often betrayed a provincialism that was juxtaposed with the savoir-faire of those who had arrived at Vanderbilt from exclusive prep schools and culturally enriched experiences that were often enhanced by international travel.

While many of my classmates at Vanderbilt traveled abroad or gained experience in family practices or business-es during summer months, I returned to Fisty at the end of each winter term to earn as much as possible as a hired hand on Knott County farms. Naturally, I would spend a great deal of time with Miss Hessie, sharing my collegiate experiences and discussing my career hopes. During these interludes, I would also have the opportunity to talk with Mary Beth Atkins, who as a junior high-aged girl was already becoming a rare beauty and demonstrating impressive intel-lect. Miss Hessie so doted upon her that when the girl dropped by her teacher's house while I was there, I became for my mentor a part of the woodwork. I felt no slight by Hessie's fascination with the Mary Beth because I was equal-ly captivated.

Graduating from Vanderbilt, I took a series of jobs as a beat writer for small broadsheets in the South before talking my way into a major newspaper in the East and launching a

John T. Hagan
Springboro, OH

syndicated column. During that time I maintained periodic correspondence with Miss Hessie, who continued to provide steadfast and stalwart instruction for her pupils in Fisty.

By the time Mary Beth had reached high school age, teenagers from one-room schoolhouses were traveling by bus to the Knott County High School in Hindman. Mary Beth was becoming increasingly adroit at mathematics under Hessie's personal tutelage, and she would annually score among the top students in Kentucky in state scholarship testing. Traveling to Eastern Kentucky University to take the Scholastic Aptitude Test, she posted a 760 on the math component of the test in the spring of her junior year. Although she earned a full scholarship for mathematics studies at Miami University in Oxford, Ohio that covered tuition, books, and room and board, her family's financial state could not provide for personal expenses. Again, Miss Hessie came through, subsidizing Mary Beth's incidentals and travel costs. While an undergrad at Miami, Mary Beth competed in several Kentucky beauty contests, and with a naturally melodic voice, she honed her skills as an a cappella soloist. She progressed in her poise and presentation, eventually capturing the crown of Miss Kentucky in the competition that led to the Miss America Pageant.

Graduating cum laude from Miami University and selected to Phi Beta Kappa, Mary Beth accepted a fellowship with stipend to the Georgia Institute of Technology for her master's degree in mathematics, but she also had the challenge of the Miss America competition. Processing with relative ease through the rigors of the various performances, she found herself among the five finalists for the coveted crown.

I, in the meantime, had been following Mary Beth's career as I pursued my own with an almost obsessive dedication. Folks back home alerted me to her successes, and I was well aware that she was competing for Miss America. Meeting deadlines was hectic, and I rarely had time for a social life. My romantic relationships with women were nearly always

John T. Hagan
Springboro, OH

subordinate to my work, a phenomenon that made those relationships typically short-lived. Nevertheless, I longed to see Mary Beth's performance in person, so I wheedled two prime seats from a journalist friend with connections. For something this spectacular, however, I wanted a date with a very special woman. I hadn't talked to the one I preferred in nearly a year, and I was most apprehensive about asking her. She accepted my offer graciously, although reminding me that I had been negligent in my calls and attentions. I arranged for her flight to New York, and together we drove to Atlantic City, New Jersey.

Atlantic City was frenetic and celebratory, and negotiating traffic was a tedious exercise in orienteering, but at length we reached Boardwalk Hall. My date raised a number of questions about Miss Kentucky, and she was seemingly more curious about her than she was interested in me.

After the five finalists had completed their responses to Bert Parks' question, they were sent back stage while the judges pondered and discussed their voting. The hall was alive with the crowd's discussions and theories on who would be the next Miss America. For my own part, I was so anxious for Mary Beth that I could hardly make small talk with my date who had become completely taken with the glamour and glitz of her surroundings.

After what seemed liked hours, Parks returned to the microphone and summoned the five finalists to center stage. Displaying apparent composure, each was surely wild with anxiety. The master of ceremonies first explained the dynamics of the outcome, citing the responsibilities of the first runner-up should Miss America be unable to perform her duties. As was the protocol of the proceedings, Parks began the countdown to the Miss America crown with nerve-racking deliberation. "Fourth runner-up for the title of Miss America is...Miss Colorado!" The audience responded in polite applause, knowing that Miss Colorado would likely be privately crushed. Receiving her flowers, she stepped to the

John T. Hagan
Springboro, OH

side of Parks. "Third runner-up...Miss Wisconsin!" Again, an almost sympathetic applause ensued, and Miss Wisconsin gracefully accepted her judgment and flowers and tactfully stepped aside. "Second runner-up...Miss Maine!" As an Eastern Seaboard representative, Miss Maine seemed to gain an even more enthusiastic and empathetic applause. A hush fell over the hall, as the denouement had arrived. The next announcement would by elimination identify the new Miss America. Parks oozed theatrically as he restated the gravity of the next placement. "And now ladies and gentlemen, I give you the first runner-up for Miss America, who, as I have said, will fulfill the duties of Miss America if she is unable to do so. First runner-up...Miss Kentucky!" The applause for Mary Beth quickly melded into that for Miss Ohio, the new Miss America.

Mary Beth Adkins turned to Miss Ohio and graciously congratulated her before the other three finalists joined her. Crowned by the previous year's Miss America, the new Miss America commenced her victory promenade on the runway as Parks began his signature song, "There she is, Miss America. There she is, your ideal..."

My heart went out to Mary Beth, even though her experience was so singular that legions of young women in America would likely have ached for her opportunity. I was resolved to talk to her backstage, and after appealing to an event official's sentimentality regarding my hometown connection with Miss Kentucky, he conducted my date and me to the area where the contestants had assembled after the ceremony.

When Mary Beth saw us, she burst into tears, not from disappointment but from exquisite joy. She virtually sailed around and through the assembly and greeted Miss Hessie Pennix, who engulfed her in her arms in such a maternal way that it nearly silenced all discourse in the room. Practically everyone divined at once that the woman in whose embrace Mary Beth was wrapped was her life's inspiration.

John T. Hagan
Springboro, OH

Mary Beth had many obligations that night and had limited time with us. Coming so close to the Miss America crown only to fall tantalizingly short was obviously painful, but knowing that the paragon of humanity, who had taken her so far in her still very young life and who had imbued in her a reverence for her roots, was present to see her on this special night was the balm of disappointment. While I felt briefly like a fifth wheel in our reunion, Mary Beth turned and thanked me in such an emotive manner that I inferred an appreciation not only for bringing Miss Hessie but in rekindling ties that traced themselves to a sterling woman and a humble schoolhouse in Fisty, Kentucky.

In spite of periodic updates about her from lifelong friends in Fisty, I all but lost track of Mary Beth over time. Nine years after the pageant, Miss Hester Pennix slept away in her reading chair in the bungalow that had become symbolic of her kindness, wisdom, and pedagogy. A dog-eared copy of Charlotte Bronte's *Jane Eyre* lay in her lap.

Attending Miss Hessie's funeral along with a host of others, I encountered a breath-taking blond who was now Dr. Mary Beth Adkins, professor of finite mathematics at Northwestern University. She had touched me on the arm at the gravesite, and said, "Long time, no see!"

Eschewing the crush of humanity assembled at the community center after the funeral, Mary Beth and I had lunch together at the Koffee Kup in town. When she mentioned that she was still unmarried, I queried tastelessly and tongue-in-cheek, "You're not gonna be another Hessie Pennix, are ya?"

Wryly, she answered, "I should be so honored, but if the right guy came along..."

Finishing her thought with a Cheshire-cat smile, I bargained, "I may just know the perfect gent."

*"Saint Joan of Arc" essay, 1904

Lou Roach
Poynette, WI

Covenant

To make a friend is a blessing.
To be a friend is a promise.

Keeping friendship strong is to delight
in the company of the other,
unafraid to be one's truest self,
listening closely to what is said,
as well as hearing what is not,
then reflecting on the message.

Friends accept one another as they are,
acknowledging differences as well as
similarities—and do not demand change.
They understand the meaning of trust,
confiding cherished dreams, foolish faux pas,
painful incidents from their pasts—
and know happiness in the sharing.

As two people learn rapport and respect,
they grow into that valued state of
reciprocity—the equal exchange
of concern with no need to question,
To find a friend is to find belonging—
unconditional welcome waiting—
a kindred heart.

Kate Leigh
Portsmouth, NH

Wind Along the Piscataqua River

The wind plays outside the house,
Chasing its tail like a spring squirrel.
Through the windows, as we walk
From room to room, we see it whirl
A dried leaf against the pane,
Then drop it quickly and be off.
The treetops near the river
Quiver, their limbs wave aloft.
We are low, the trees are high,
Above us is the weathered sky,
The north wind drives her crowded
Lavender fleece cloud-drifts on by.
November dies a trembling
Death with this tricky wind beset.
December fluffs frosty skirts,
Puffs her wintery ice-tinged breath.
The sun's strength recedes and leaves
Us yearning for her generous heat.
Summer's a memory now, she's
Tiptoed out on her flip-flopped feet.

David Campbell
Cape Elizabeth, ME

Woodworks

1
I profit from destruction, turning
a neighbor's tree discards to firewood.
Easy splitting among the oak butts,
inhaling their medicine-chest camphor,
laying out like filleted fish
the straight white meat of maple,
the dry poplar that almost splits itself.

Elm is trouble, even sawn
to midget lengths, a bottomless pit
of double helix heartwood sinews
clutching wedges tighter
the deeper I drive and sweat—
hell-bent on defeating
steel and man: succeeding.

2
Choosing 2x4s in the lumberyard,
we reject those that reject us
by writhing, twisting, bending
out of the orderly stacked cubes.
I admire them, northern mavericks
of pine, spruce, fir; they survived
the ovens untamed and will not stand
as studs or lie down as base plates.
They had their own home and want it back.

David Campbell
Cape Elizabeth, ME

Their bad behavior is a homing
no less than that of birds and fish,
becoming propeller blades
to fly back into the mother trunk,
the native ground, the dance
of spiraling, pliant wands
from great below to great above.
That's the homesick longing
of all the useless 2x4s.

3.
A circle of small chamfered spires
leans out of the leaf bed. The pine trunk
they buttressed fed this forest long ago,
and they play dead inside a desiccated
film of gray camouflage. I scrape
with a jackknife and meet sticky orange
and a whiff of turpentine.

So is this death, a flambeau
keeping snug its nascent fire?
But nothing cools its heels in this
hotbed of rebirth, where stillness
amplifies the drinking down of light
and fluid upsurge, where I'm a middleman
angling, rummaging between.

Mollie Schmidt
Rome, ME

Calling

I yearn for summer nights,
windows wide to the western wind—
I listen for the loons.

One moans now across the water,
yearning, calling for a mate,
voicing a sad, lonesome sound.

Finally an answer cry comes
from far down the lengthy lake;
the first loon goes madly into

a delirium of arpeggios,
and I am amused, and glad,
and lonely.

***

Metaphor

Earth falls away as I become airborne,
pointed up, the wide sky my road,
climbing the clouds til they drop
beneath, then the blue, breathtaking bank
to level flight. Voices crackle
in my ears, but beyond their scope, I'm
lost like a dot with no dimension,
traveling a line toward home.
Thought suspended, I give myself
to the bumpy air sensation,
trusting myself to risk a fall,
or transformation.

Goose River Anthology, 2013//22

Janice Babcock
Wauwatosa, WI

Long Lake Fisheree...Then and Now

Over fifty years ago, I remember being invited to come to an ice fishing Fisheree with my parents, Connie and Delbert. My aunt and uncle, Reuben and Bernice, lived on Long Lake in Wisconsin. They invited us up to see a Fisheree. For many summers, I had been water skiing and swimming in the sparkling water of Long Lake. However, that special January 1961 weekend, my parents and I were being exposed to the magic of ice fishing on a clear winter day in Wisconsin.

Ice fishing was a unique adventure for me. We were garbed in our winter duds, including jackets, caps and warm leather gloves to shield us from the sharp wind. I was an ice queen, wearing a special red, white and blue Icelandic style woolen sweater hand-knit for me by Mom. It was warm and cozy.

Uncle Reuben and Aunt Bernice showed us around by visiting other fishing shanties and meeting their fellow fishing friends. Then we headed to the adventure at hand.

Reuben's primitively-heated fishing hut located in the middle of frozen Long Lake, not too far from his fishing pier, now provided our hideaway. The fishing holes had previously been drilled through the deep ice. Fishing inside the shanty consisted of using cut-off fishing rods to accommodate the tiny fishing space in the corners of the shanty. We sat on wood lawn chairs while wearing winter coats. Ha! We dangled my uncle's alluring baits from a short rod to attract and hopefully catch fish swimming below that glistening snow and ice.

Of course, part of the ambiance with ice fishing was snacking. We had locally made Wisconsin cheese from the neighboring cheese factory to go with crackers. My aunt offered us her time-consuming, hand-shelled nuts from area hickory trees which are gathered in late fall. We also had

Janice Babcock
Wauwatosa, WI

potato chips with liquid refreshments. While settling in to serious fishing, we talked, shared our stories and jokes, and laughed. Occasionally another angler stopped by to check how our fishing was going. All in all, we were having simple fun on a frosty day.

Eventually, we left the shanty and walked down to check on the status of current anglers at the Fisheree. Gosh, what a cadre of caught fish, including walleye, northern pike, bass, crappies, bluegill and perch. We speculated on the potential winners.

Unfortunately, my relatives did not catch any fish on that outing. Not to worry! That evening, Aunt Bernice pan-fried her Long Lake fish caught and frozen earlier. In their cozy year-round lake home, we indulged in culinary pleasures that melted in our mouth. What family fun we had!

About fifty years later, I was remembering my 1961 Fisheree experience. I called and inquired if a Fisheree was coming up. Yes! I had the pleasure of talking to a local restaurant owner. He immediately remembered my aunt and uncle. His family had a long heritage of owning land on the Long Lake. We swapped stories. He encouraged me to come and attend the Long Lake Fisheree in Northern Kettle Moraine State Forest.

He proposed that I shop for the traction steel coils that attach to my boots for safer walking on the ice or packed snow. He told me I would find tent enclosures with food for sale with winter camaraderie. There would be a display of the fish caught and a tub with the fish that would be released at the end of the Fisheree.

I wanted to go, even though my other four of our original team had passed away. I returned and an acquaintance drove me down a steep incline from the road to the lake. Being in a car on lake ice was scary for me. I remembered TV news reports of cars breaking through lake ice. Out of the car, I gingerly walked around on the snow with that traction device over my boots. Other than that, it seemed to me ice

Janice Babcock
Wauwatosa, WI

fishing hadn't changed much. I saw ardent anglers tending their tip-ups. Even their dogs romping around on the ice sparked enthusiasm. Ice fishing activity highlighted unique custom-made fish shanties and added harmony to the adventure.

In Wisconsin a winter walk on the lake with its trees and glistening ice offers a special lure. Speaking to the winter fishing zealots heightened my enthusiasm for their sport. I renewed my passion for the simple pleasure of seeing fish caught below that frozen sheet of thick ice and winter fun. It offers a feast for the senses in every way!

I enjoyed coming back. But most of all, I could cherish memories of my youth more than fifty years ago.

First published in *The Statesman*, Kewaskum, WI, 2011.

***

Laureen Haben, OSF
Milwaukee, WI

Bird Work

In summer
last year's amaryllis plants
sit in the sun
to nurture new buds.
House wrens steal beakfuls
of the protective moss
along with scraps of paper,
sometimes
three and four pieces at a time.
We can tell when
they are housekeeping.

Judith Canty Graves
Wayland, MA

A Face Across the Room

In a room full of people,
I looked as someone spoke.
A woman said her name to all of us,
but it wasn't her name that I recognized.
I recognized her soul first,
then gradually her face.
Could this really be the person
I had known twenty-five years ago?
Her face, so different now,
showed the passing of the years.
I remembered her youthful expression and energy.
Now she looked fatigued and somber.
Did she recognize me from across the room?
Perhaps I also look
very different to others.
Although we had known each other briefly
in another time and place,
I still knew her despite the years.
Time did not matter.
I wondered: has her life been hard?
Has she struggled?
She looks different now,
yet I recognized her in a sea of faces.
It was a soul connection across a crowded room.

Sylvia Little-Sweat
Wingate, NC

Homecoming

A cross breeze from the open
windows of the country church
carried the scent of starched shirts
men's hair tonic and aftershave
ladies' powder and perfume.
Like a shadow at noon I clung
to Mother's side waiting to taste
the fried chicken, the stacked cake
Mother had packed in Grandma's
basket. Dinner on the grounds
would soon take place in the oaks'
deep shade near the big silver bell
rung in bygone days to call men
from their fields to dig new graves.

I shared the dark, polished pew
with a few of Mother's friends
to sing bent-on-Heaven hymns
and remember all those Sundays
when Mother sang in the choir.
Lifting our joyful Gospel sound,
could we penetrate the peace
or the silence of the adjoining
burial ground where Mother
lay at last by Daddy's side?
With mallet force the August
sun by noon would drum again
a muted tune on the hard-baked
clay of her nine-months' grave.

Diane Reitz
Winter Park, FL

Happy Endings

sitting on the front porch with Dad
or around the pool with Nana
having conversations
flowing like water
downhill easy and delightful

absorbing a little along
the way and taking
to heart what I could,
understanding as the voices
traveled down their road
of experience to my house

with hope, always hope
floating down the hill too.
great expectations topping
problems as a cherry on top
of the dark chocolate sauce
with unknown outcomes.

now the porch is not ours
the pool, strangers under umbrellas,
voices have grown silent
except the memories of them
still play music in my mind
floating notes down to my heart

just one more pretty conversation
under a tree, near the fireplace
even from a hospital bed
would soften my soul and
keep hope in place for my
yearnings for a tomorrow

Diane Reitz
Winter Park, FL

reading through the chapters
pushing to get to the happy ending

looking for the happy endings.

***

Story Time

Unlike our ruins of old
stories unfold
and grow more famous
stronger and robust

Stories passed along
like celestial songs
carry the family history
past generation's mystery

We are what is told
No matter how old
The children want to hear
Our songs of past years

So have your story time
each night before bed
and tell them quietly—the tales
of all that was said

Joyce Pye
Bath, ME

The Devil's Ache

We sweat together those midsummer days—
Backs bent like brothers by the Devil's Ache
While Pleasant River valley, steeped in haze,
Became the promised land; we set our stake
And planted sixteen years in fertile soil.

The marsh grass sweet with cricket song at night
Allayed all fears a stranger might despoil
Our peace. Yet, sudden as an autumn blight
The Census Man—blurry eye, shaky hand—
Stood at the door: with pride I named my kin.
Darcy and Tom would one day claim this land:
We read, and write our family name: Sherbin.

But in that Census book our name's below
Judge Benham's.....writ in ink: *Sherbourne, Negro*

Roger M. Woodbury
Morrill, ME

Haying

When I was a boy my family went to Maine every summer. We went to see my grandmother and grandfather and stayed in their cottage. My sister was five and a half years older and she never missed an opportunity to emphasize it.

Just up the road was my great uncle Ralph's farm. Uncle Ralph was retired but he always had a couple of cows and some chickens. Up in back of the big white farmhouse were two big fields that grew hay for winter feed for the cows. In August there was always hay to be gathered and put up in his big barn.

Every Monday my mother would drive up to my grandmother's house to do the laundry. Sometimes she and my grandmother would bake bread and rolls, or even cookies which was better. Mother would do the laundry in the big, round, brass-colored ringer washing machine with its odd-looking exposed electric motor on the bottom that made such strange noises as it turned the wheel-like agitator inside the tub back and forth. Usually when Mother went to Gramma's on Monday, she would take me with her, even those times when I didn't want to go. It was boring at Gramma's because my grandfather was still working and the woods up the hill in back of the house were dark and deep for me, the city kid.

There were chickens in a chicken coop, but they weren't very interesting for long, and I was told never to play on the old tractor in Grampa's garage. The only thing I could do was sit on the big, cement front step and look across the road at the big sawmill, listening to the whine of the big saw as it cut logs into boards. One day I saw a truck loaded with boards fall over as it tried to drive out of the mill. That was pretty exciting but I never saw that happen again.

One day when I was six, Uncle Ralph came to the house and took me back to his farm with him. He drove a very old,

Roger M. Woodbury
Morrill, ME

rusty, Model A Ford pickup that had holes in the floorboards. Uncle Ralph had severe arthritis in both knees and walked with two canes unless he was in his truck. He took me out into the big back field and taught me how to use a pitchfork that morning. The hay had been rolled into long rows and it was my job to take the pitch fork with its four, long, thin tines and flip the rows of hay over so they would dry in the sun. Uncle Ralph told me my job was most important because the hay needed to be dry in order to be put up. He showed me how to hold the pitch fork, with its long, hand-made handle that was longer than I was tall. He showed me to hold it just so. It was easy and he said I was good at it. He said, "Mebbe bineby you kin help pick up the hay an' put it on Harry's waggin' when we're puttin' it bye." Uncle Ralph and Grampa both talked like that and it took about half the summer before I really knew what they were saying every time.

I asked if the "waggin" was going to be pulled by his truck, because I knew the rake that made the hay lines was pulled by the truck. I had seen him driving the truck pulling the big, iron-wheeled rake, my sister sitting on the seat of the rake. Every once in a while he'd push down on a pedal that tipped the big hay rake up to release the gathered hay.

"No," Uncle Ralph said. "Ole Harry's comin' with his hoss and waggin. The waggin's too big for this truck."

"Can I come and help?" I asked.

"Well," he said, "you ask your mother." I vowed that the next Monday I would go up to Uncle Ralph's and help hay. After all, I knew how to use a pitch fork and Uncle Ralph said I was good at it.

That next Monday, Mother and Gramma told me they were going to bake some cookies. They said I could have some with milk "bine bye." I had other plans. I was going to go haying.

My sister had stayed overnight with Gramma and Grampa. She did that quite a lot in the summer. She wasn't

Roger M. Woodbury
Morrill, ME

there that day. My grandfather wasn't either. They were both up to Uncle Ralph's haying. I knew Ole Harry was going to be there with his "hoss and waggin" and I was going to be there, too. Cookies and milk held no charm for me that afternoon.

I marched into the kitchen where Mother and Gramma were and announced that I was going to go up to Uncle Ralph's and hay.

"Oh, I don't know, Rog," said Mother.

"We're goin t'have cookies and milk afore long," said Gramma. "You don't want to miss that now, do you?"

"Yes, I want to go hay. Ole Harry's coming with his hoss and waggin. Last week Uncle Ralph showed me how and I want to go and hay. He said I could," I stated as proof.

There was a little argument. It was about half a mile up the road to Uncle Ralph's farm. My mother didn't want me to go wandering off alone. My grandmother was concerned because the "cahs went so fahst gwin down stritt." But in the end, I got my way.

"You stay way over t'edge of the rud, now. Them cahs there go awful fahst down that rud," said Gramma. I remember my mother just sort of fussed. I promised to watch for the "fahst cahs" carefully and started walking along the gravel shoulder: I was going haying at last!

Uncle Ralph's house was at the end of a long curving driveway. It was a big, white farm house with a large, three story barn on the end. The ground sloped down toward the road from the house so it was necessary to walk all the way up the driveway and around to the back before coming to the big field that went way out to the woods in back.

I walked a long way into the field smelling the hay and hearing the click of crickets before I could see the hay wagon that had with rubber tires as if from a truck. It was being pulled by a big, black horse. I saw four people walking beside and one riding on the back of the wagon. As I walked across the field and drew closer, I saw that each worker would pitch

Roger M. Woodbury
Morrill, ME

a fork holding hay up over the side of the wagon and the person on the wagon would stick his fork down to hold the hay so the first fork could be removed. There was a kind of simple rhythm I could see. I saw my sister raising a pitch fork, and my grandfather also. My great-uncle Ralph, with his bad arthritis, worked along with everyone, using his pitchfork as first a cane, then a pitchfork as the wagon moved slowly along. I heard the wagon and horse's leather harness creak. I heard the swoosh of hay being pitched up.

On top of the hay pile on the wagon was a boy my sister's age. He stabbed the fork-loads of hay as they were pitched up. I found out his uncle was Ole Harry, who was kneeling on the hay in the front of the wagon holding the reigns of his black horse. He seemed to be a very old man. He wore a red-checkered, long-sleeved shirt, overalls, and a broad-brimmed straw hat not unlike my grandfather and uncle wore. He seemed sort of hunched over on the hay.

My sister was the first to see me walking across the field. She stopped her work and looked at me, hissing, "What do you want?" My sister considered our grandfather and great-uncle Ralph to be her personal property. Whenever I came close she did whatever she could to send me away.

In as big and loud a voice as I could muster I announced, "I've come to help hay!" There was a lot of laughter. My sister turned away with a gesture of disgust. I remember my grandfather saying, "Oh, gorrie. I don't know, Rog." I felt the hesitation like an invisible fog coming from everyone. It made me feel hot down my back and I felt my underpants stick to me. It seemed I was intruding on a secret party.

It was "Old Harry" who saved my day. "Well, now, I cud use some hep up here drivin' this old hoss. Why'nt you come up heah on this waggin, and hep me drive this hoss?"

Those were the days when Roy Rogers and Trigger and the Lone Ranger and Silver were the biggest heroes imaginable. I really wanted to hold a pitch fork like Uncle Ralph had taught me. I wanted to pitch the hay up onto the wagon and

Roger M. Woodbury
Morrill, ME

show my sister I knew how to do it and I really thought standing up on top of the "waggin" and "catching" the hay being pitched up from the ground was probably one of the best jobs to have...ever. But at that moment, nothing was as good as the prospect of actually driving that "hoss!"

I climbed up on the wagon, stepping on the hub of the front wheel, then the top of the tire before Ole Harry pulled me up beside him by my arm. There was no seat. Instead we perched on our knees on the hay pile, Ole Harry, holding the thick, leather reigns that ran down to the horse. It seemed as though we were a mile in the air looking down at that horse's back. At first for me it was scary. I smelled the combined odor of big horse, old wood wagon, fresh hay and Ole Harry's chewing tobacco.

Ole Harry said, "Gyup." The horse snorted and started his plodding walk pulling the wagon and the rhythm of haying resumed.

Ole Harry let me hold the reigns!

The hay pile in the wagon grew taller as more and more of the hay got pitched up. The horse plodded back and forth in the field.

I got to hold the reigns!

Ole Harry looked down at me, and started to laugh. I remember looking at his weathered face and his mostly toothless grin as he said to me, "Fust time on m' knees in m'life, boy!" He cackled harder at his little joke.

I laughed, too. After all, he let me hold the reigns.

Before long the wagon was lurching down the field toward Uncle Ralph's barn. Beyond the woods, I heard a grumble of thunder and there were big, dark gray clouds gathering their strength for a late afternoon thunderstorm. Long raindrops started to fall as the horse and wagon went into the barn so the hay could be forked up into the loft.

I drove by Uncle Ralph's place yesterday afternoon. It was an afternoon not unlike the one when I was six. The Surry Road is much wider now. I could hear my grandmother war-

Roger M. Woodbury
Morrill, ME

ing me that "the cahs go awful fahst." Indeed they do.

The old house burned down after Uncle Ralph died years ago. All that's left now is the driveway, overgrown with weeds and grass. I walked up to the field, surprised to see some men haying near the woods.

No "hoss" and no "waggin" now. No pitchforks flashing in the afternoon sun. Instead a truck pulled a long red machine that gulped hay and spit out wire-tight bales. No sound reached me across the field.

Above, angry-looking clouds clustered. I closed my eyes and smelled fresh hay. A grumble of early thunder and suddenly again I smelled that big, black horse and Ole Harry's tobacco. I felt again the lurch of his "waggin." I heard the clink of the fork tines, the swoosh of the hay and the crickets.

For a moment, that day I was six and went haying was real again.

***

Robert Erickson
Round Pond, ME

Pictures

My eyes have captured the shoreline soft
And the vast blue sky reeling gulls aloft
The ocean greys deeply following a misty rain
Pictures perfect of this creation called Maine

Julia Rice
Milwaukee, WI

The Secrets

Remember when secrets were pleasant,
when giggles leaped into corners
and excitement tap-danced down our veins
and words heard in whispers
morphed into silly sentences,
when we sat around a birthday cake,
crumbs marching toward our plates,
ice cream rolling round raised edges.

Now the secrets hover in the dark,
offspring of the pain of children,
threatening the very air outside,
moist and murky in the streetlight.
Fear whispers distortions.
Hatred lurks in the veins of strangers.

Laughter mocks the ears of the hearer
who fears the word that twists the truth
and chokes the twisted whispers
that shocked and thrilled the child.
The drink burns even as it quenches the terror.

Mary Ellen Stypinski
Harpswell, ME

Anniversary Pantoum

The warmth of the hearth welcomes us
We gaze at the radiant flames' elusive hues
Beckoning us to sit beside the fire
Fire speaks; embers spark in rhythm

We gaze at the radiant flames' elusive hues
As we toast to celebrate our union
Fire speaks; embers spark in rhythm
While we reflect on the life we've shared

As we toast to celebrate our union
Simple pleasures produce vivid memories
While we reflect on the life we've shared
Rich dark chocolate compliments the wine

Simple pleasures produce vivid memories
Reliving blessed moments and peaceful times
Rich dark chocolate compliments the wine
Soft music brings pleasure to our ears

Reliving blessed moments and peaceful times
We dream of a secure future together
Soft music brings pleasure to our ears
Wooden logs are furnished to fuel the blaze

We dream of a secure future together
Desiring a bountiful harvest in golden years
Wooden logs are furnished to fuel the blaze
The warmth of the hearth delights us

Mary Ellen Stypinski
Harpswell, ME

Desiring a bountiful harvest in golden years
We see our fortune in the embers glow
The warmth of the hearth delights us
As we renew the promise of our endless love

We see our fortune in the embers glow
Beckoning us to sit beside the fire
As we renew the promise of our endless love
The warmth of the hearth welcomes us

***

Steve Troyanovich
Florence, NJ

Christmas Eve Poem

the world is new tonight
seeking its way back to eden
dreams fill your eyes...

lingering in the lonesome valley
of the lost solstice moon
little stars slumber in silvery farawayness
cradled by a snowman's remembrance
of glistening winter winds
filled with peppermint petals...

touch me now... immerse me
in your tender nakedness
i would leave this place
remembering only dazzling snowflower orchards
and the loving mantle of tomorrow's bride
where the fawn sleeps still...

Goose River Anthology, 2013//39

Carol Leavitt Altieri
Madison, CT

El Dorado

Holding my new baby girl, time stops. I carry her
down to the sand from a courtyard
by the sea. With thundering waves coming
in, we breathe the invigorating air off the ocean.

Alicia, in a state of grace captures
me by her eyes,
lifting her head to see
her mother. A soul, a heart, rosy-pink
body, a tiny mouth, with my skin
and father's blue eyes.

Perched in a core of nursing arms,
she is embraced with uneasy happiness,
a microcosm of all that is perfect
and vulnerable.
I hope to possess a secret amulet
that will protect her from life's monster traps.

We breathe together, I stare at her,
and see the sea reflected in her eyes
as she unfolds a morning's radiance
like the rare bird, the Indigo Bunting.

She smiles in the sanctuary of my cradling
as I sing a roundelay of love.

First published in *Chronicles of Humans With Nature,*
Goose River Press, 2013.

Todd R. Nelson
Wallingford, PA

The Vizier of Native Brook Trout

Ed is the Vizier of Brook Trout in our smalltown in Maine. And now that the water level is high with the spring run off, the beaver dam flowage swollen, the brook's running in spate as the ice in the lakes dissipates, the water temperature inching upward with every sunny day, it is time for me to ask Ed if he will reveal another of his secret fishing holes.

I am beguiled by the stories of myth and legend: of Ed herding 14 inch brook trout right over beaver dams and into his creel with only a few articulate whistles; calling trout by name to move them from pool to pool, lest they fall into undeserving hands; guiding *those deemed worthy* to his secret spots blindfolded, by night, in the interest of sanctity and preservation. I could go on. I am told he has photos encapsulating some extraordinary days of fishing on the local streams. But *which* streams—that will always be the question.

He guards them assiduously, cautious about divulging too much of an activity that has taken on the aspect of a life's work, of conservation verging on guardianship. After many months of discussion and prompting, Ed gave me actual directions, not allusions, to a fishing spot. Not, alas, with the aid of a map. This was a challenge. His reference points are vague, or colloquial. Directions such as "turn left where Andy Snow used to live, then go along 'til you see that big spruce that was struck by lighting last summer. . . the fishing hole is in the brook just below there" do not always do the trick. Perhaps Ed is aware of that.

He talks with much more exacting fervor and detail about his own excursions and tantalizing successes. "I could have caught my limit last Sunday," he has told me. "By golly, weren't they just jumping onto the hook yesterday," he has told me. "I caught the biggest brook trout that you ever laid

Todd R. Nelson
Wallingford, PA

eyes on just standing on the beaver dam down by. . ." he has told me, before lapsing into directions to the dam that I can only find useless. Perhaps Ed is aware of that.

I suppose I am his "sport," in the old Maine guide usage: the sportsman from "away" who needs help gaining proximity to wild quarry. Before making Ed's acquaintance, I would spend hours driving to fishing spots due to the "received wisdom" that one had to enter the next county inland from the coast of Penobscot Bay before finding worthwhile trout fishing. Ed has changed my mind about that. The peculiar, unlikely streams abounding within a twenty minute walk of Andy Snow's, as it turns out, are flush with the most beautiful, iridescent, lively and skeptical native fish. This has made me a fan of local, humble waters.

Last summer, on the basis of a relatively clear set of directions from Ed, my son and I went in search of "the stone bridge fishing spot," the one at which, Ed said, a rather goofy and social black bear once sat on the opposite bank watching him fish. The deer flies devoured Spencer and me on the walk through the woods, but sure enough we located the spot: a beautiful, diminutive pond behind a beaver dam, steeply bounded on all sides by tall spruce trees; ducks gliding among the lily pads in shallow water; the outlet spilling over a bouldered walkway, the "stone bridge," below which the stream gurgled its way south. The fish were jumpin' and the water was high. No goofy bear, alas. We fished happily— but unsuccessfully. . . we were fishing, not catching—for an hour, and then retreated up the trail as a warm summer rain dimpled the pond. It was worth the deer flies.

It has taken me a while, but I did finally achieve Ed's actual company for an afternoon of fishing. I offered to be blindfolded and spun around before the walk to the "secret spot," and he seemed to consider it seriously. And it was a sign of deep trust, I guess, that I was not blindfolded nor even sworn to silence. Or perhaps it was just a sign of the relative value of the spot to which he guided me. This day might

Todd R. Nelson
Wallingford, PA

have been a test of worthiness. We were beginning on the bottom rung of trout lairs, I suspected.

So one sunny day we scouted a small brook, jumping from bank to bank, sneaking up on potential pools so as not to scare the wily brookies. Ed perceived fishy nests in unusual places. We "flogged"' the quick waters, I with dry flies and Ed with a number eight hook and a worm. And it was as if he called the fish by name, the way they came to his lure—fish after fish, each greeted by the Vizier with an affectionate "hello darling," like an old friend, each fish gently returned to its home with a respectful toss. As it turned out, my afternoon was nothing but casting practice. Evidently, there is more to the fishing relationship than being acquainted with the right spot. Native fish respond differently to native fishermen, or is it vice versa. Perhaps Ed knows that. Perhaps this year he will tell me the secret password.

***

Kate Leigh
Portsmouth, NH

Prayer Flags

The prayer flags flap chill,
Their colors, vibrant, visible.
Skeletal trees clatter so,
Wasted weeds in winds blow.
Snark cold curls my hands,
Barren pack spread the sand.
Far away lone train whistle,
Nearby dried tattered thistle.
Prayer flags skittish-wave,
All the rest, nature's slave.

Lorelee L. Sienkowski
Packwaukee, WI

Christmas, 1861

The chaplain came through No-Man's-Land;
it almost got him killed.
He brought with him a flag of truce
'cross fields that once was tilled.

"I came to help you bury dead,
God knows you've got enough,
We've had our share, your guys are good,
But both are kinda tough.

I know you got no chaplain,
You've sung no Sunday songs,
so here am I to help you pray
o'er dead laid deep and long."

We dug their graves and laid them out,
we tried to write their names.
Some we remembered rightly,
but most had died unclaimed.

So many died around them
that not one memory's left,
but rosters hold a counting
and names whose families' cleft.

We buried all the dead ones,
the lame we sent away,
the shattered and the grieving
fought on another day.

Lorelee L. Sienkowski
Packwaukee, WI

The chaplain went back 'cross the lines
but shared his message first:
'bout loving God and Peace on Earth
and waters quenching thirst.

We shared our grits and 'baccy
we shared our weevily bread
we thanked him for his caring
and blessing all our dead.

***

Autumn Sumac Sunsets

Autumn sumac sunsets:
burnt orange against turquoise green.
The end of summer's indolence—
the respite 'fore weather that's mean.

I relish the calm days of autumn
warm days and the crisp evening air.
Time to settle and find a warm burrow;
stock up the garden's fall fare.

With food in the larder,
with quilts on the bed,
and books to be savored
whenever they're read
I can handle the prospect
of harsh days ahead,
when memory remembers
green, orange and red.

Ann M. Penton
Green Valley, AZ

Author! Author!

Mystifying:
In many dreams,
I'm reading something
out of a book I hold.

Frustrating:
Rarely can I hang onto
the content upon awakening.

The puzzle:
Do I have photo-etched copies of
some old book stored inside my skull,
ready for replay?

Are there books available in sleep-time,
just as there are blue convertibles to drive,
apricot juice to spill, kittens that pounce,
and picnic tables?

In English? Or some other language?
Or just gibberish that feels fine?

Or—and this is what I *really* wonder:
am I making it up as I go, as fast as I read,
and just a step ahead?
Is it a great novel? an intricate mystery?
a profoundly moving poem?

And how could I get a copy?

Bill Tucker
Aurora, OH

Ghost Stories

When I think of things that happened when I was a kid, I get confused about what happened first. A lot of the details get mixed up, and the people I knew intrude into my memory where they couldn't have been at all. For instance, I remember sitting on the curb with my brother, Billy, telling ghost stories when I was eight or nine years old. But about that time I remember burning leaves in the street, and the street was gravel, so there wasn't any curb for us to sit on. And Billy couldn't have been there, either; he died when I was six.

But I know Simon was there, and Duane, who always sat in the middle, because he was oldest, except for Simon, who didn't count. I know Gary and Flora and the Sumrall brothers. Dan and Howell, were there and Gregg and Marilyn, who always sat together, even then. Of course I was there, sitting on the end (because I was youngest), hugging my trembling knees.

We always sat in front of Gary's house because of the comfort of the streetlight. It was over a block from where I lived, and sometimes I tried to get them to come to my house. They did once, but sitting in the dark was unbearable. We couldn't even see each other, and the fear was too personal.

Simon was an imbecile. His mother took him out of school about the time I was born, and in all those years he just played around the house or followed her wherever she went. She couldn't let him out of her sight. Whenever she was in town you could always see Simon loping along after her. If you saw Simon looking at the toys in the window of the dime store, you could look around and see his mother talking to some other woman or just standing close by with her eye on him, waiting for him to get through looking.

For a long time she wouldn't let Simon go as far as Gary's

Bill Tucker
Aurora, OH

at night, unless she was going to sit on the front porch and talk to Gary's folks. That way she could watch him and take him home when he got scared. I've often wondered why she let him sit and listen to the gory tales we made up. They tormented me at night when I was lying in bed, incapable of keeping my mind from going over and over each macabre detail. The phantoms I made of the moonlit branches outside my windows caused me to draw the shades and cower in darkness. And I know how they must have affected Simon, and, looking back, I realize how much more terrifying they must have been in the dark corridors of that crippled brain. But I can also see the mute pleading of those imbecile eyes and the agony of compassion in hers. So she let him come and share our torment, because she had forgotten, if she had ever known, what the terror of ghost stories was like.

Then a summer came—I was ten and Simon was twenty—when she let him go that far at night alone. Perhaps his anguished cries no longer brought her from her bed at night, or maybe her ready, comforting words could calm him to sleep, or she may have become too wearied by the constant vigil. His hugeness—he was bigger than any man I had even seen—may have reassured her that he would be safe. So he came alone and sat and listened in the thin incandescent safety of the light.

Simon lived directly across the street from me, and it was comforting to have his great hulk beside me when we came home at night. Even while I tried to calm him, I was aware of the great strength in his broad back, and the human mass of him insulated me from the mystery of the night.

Simon was not afraid of any real danger. Between Gary's house and mine the Shroeders' dark patch of shrubbery-shadowed lawn held the menace of a snarling mongrel dog. I could feel, when I did not hear, the violent rush as he burst from his hiding place to bark and threaten as we passed. But to Simon this puny dog was nothing compared to the wall-clinging Dracula that Flora had conjured up before him.

Bill Tucker
Aurora, OH

His step would not falter as we passed, and, as if affronted, the dog would bark and threaten the more, until one night a spasm of unbearable rage drove his mouth to Simon's legs. Without a sound or hesitation Simon buried his foot in the dog's stomach so that all threat was wrung from the infuriated throat in a single, short yelp of pain. And Simon walked on without a backward glance at the barely breathing furry lump that it would take two months of anxious care to make into a dog again. So I stopped carrying the stick that was to be my protection against this little beast, and instead walked across the street to fetch Simon from his mother and take him with me as my armor.

I grew to like this man-boy in a proud and protective way, and his mother came to look upon me as something of a guardian. I pridefully accepted the responsibility of determining when he was to be spared a certain tale and sometimes urged him from the curb to take him home, only to return for the grotesque story myself.

But without him beside me the sudden slap of some unknown steps in the dark or an unfamiliar sound from across the street would bring my racing heart into my throat and send me skittering toward the yellow light-island, my sanctuary of fear under the telephone pole a block away.

Someone might say, "What's the matter, Red? What you running for? Feel old Dracula crawling up your back?"

Because that was exactly what I had felt, I could only grin and sit down and become lost in the new story.

I was not the only one who cast glances over his shoulder into the darkness or listened intently for some sound other than the storytelling voice. Nor was I the only one who preferred to sit cross-legged in the gutter rather than be too far out on the unprotected end of the shivering line of children huddled there on the curb. When a night moth fluttered against the hanging bare lightbulb and our little yellow world darkened momentarily, I didn't shudder alone.

One night late in summer—when early fallen sycamore

Bill Tucker
Aurora, OH

leaves were blown along the dark gutter to brush against our vulnerable and skinny legs, and the chill of autumn was in the air—we sat and told our stories. Perhaps the melancholy of the lost summer was with us all, for we shivered more than could be accounted for by the invoked spirits and coolness of the night.

Earlier than other evenings Simon began to quiver and shake. The low moaning that started, baritone and resonant, deep in his man's chest, and that would break, as always, into an aggravating, monotonic whimper, came after a preliminary and unfrightening account of Gregg's trip through the graveyard. This so provoked Duane that he dug a sharp elbow into Simon's ribs and gibingly asked, "What's the matter, Simon? You scared of that graveyard?"

"Leave him alone, Duane," Flora rebuked, "You'll just make him worse."

"He'll be bellowing so loud in a minute we'll all have to go home," Duane protested, resenting the challenge to his authority.

"You just leave him alone," Flora repeated.

This was unusual for her. From time to time Simon had received pokes and prods and shaming remonstrances from all of us to bring him back to our little circle of reality. At other times there was nothing but torment for Simon as a motive for the comments and suggestions offered by us all. In our childish cruelty we would make every situation more horrible and whisper an embroidery of dreadful detail into Simon's recoiling ear.

But Flora was impatient with anything that would delay the telling, suspecting this might be our last night of freedom from parents and schoolroom assignments.

"Simon, you hush up," she said.

We went on with our stories, each telling his in turn. All the while Simon whimpered, and I still remember that night and hear his sound through twenty years of other babbling voices. I can still see the group, as with the eye of some

Bill Tucker
Aurora, OH

observer, huddled in exhilarated terror in the center of a yellow ring of light disturbed by a spattering of swirling moth shadows.

And as Flora produced her bloodless Frankenstein, Simon's wail went out into the darkness.

I sometimes, on looking back, credit myself with a subtle prevision of things to come that fatal night. There was suddenly within me an agitation such as I had never felt before. Perhaps there was such a note in Simon's plaintive cry as to set my ten-year-old nerves atremble. But his despondency so affected me that I suddenly stood and pulled at his arm until he finally lumbered to his feet. There was no consoling him in our block-long walk home and I delivered him, still whimpering, to his mother. When I went to bed the light still burned in Simon's room across the street.

It was Mr. Sullivan who brought Simon to our door the next morning before breakfast. Mr. Sullivan, like Simon's father, was a night-running railroad man, and he had found Simon shambling aimlessly about the railroad yard when he climbed down from the cab of his locomotive.

"I can't raise anybody over at Ferguson's," I heard him say to my father. "You better look after his boy, Frank. I have to get on home."

They talked briefly at the door, and as soon as Mr. Sullivan left, my father came in for a whispered conference with my mother. I stood concealed at the door to overhear.

"John found Simon roaming around the railroad yard," he told her.

Musingly my mother asked, "How do you suppose he got away from Ethel?"

"I don't know. You know how she watches him."

"Like a hawk. Maybe he followed Herb when he went down," my mother speculated.

This was disavowed with a shake of my father's head.

"Herb went out yesterday afternoon," he said.

"How long do you suppose he's been gone?"

Bill Tucker
Aurora, OH

My father shrugged his shoulders. I stood in full view now, and I could see him formulating his own questions behind the frown on his face.

"I wonder what he was doing down in the railroad yard?" He didn't expect an answer; he was questioning himself. For a while he stood looking out the kitchen window.

"Where is he now?" my mother asked.

"I told him to sit on the porch. I'm going over with him." He stopped as if thinking about something. "Have you heard Ethel out calling him?"

"No. And that's funny, too. Why hasn't she missed him before now?" My mother looked in mild alarm at my father.

"I don't know, with Herb out on the road. You don't suppose—" Here my father stopped as if judiciously weighing what he should say. He resumed, "Maybe you better go over with us."

I went, too, but far behind and unseen.

When they found Ethel Ferguson, my mother fainted dead away. She crumpled to the floor in a soft bundle and my father seemed almost impatient with her as he scooped her up and laid her on Simon's bed. He didn't attempt to revive her; he just returned to stare down into Mrs. Ferguson's grotesque face. She lay beside Simon's bed where he had dropped her, her nakedness apparent through her nightgown. I couldn't take my eyes from her once-pretty face that was now so horrible, as if the strangling hands still clutched the blue and swollen throat.

As we stood there—it was only a moment of mind-shocked inability to more—a low and painful moan came from Simon's throat. His hands began to twitch convulsively and his eyes fixed my father with an indescribable malevolence. He must have seen in us the murderer he couldn't remember himself to be. When he made his brutish charge my father knocked him unconscious with one blow.

What apparitions were we in the morning light of Simon's tiny brain?

Bill Tucker
Aurora, OH

I think of all this now because I have just seen Simon again. Dead in his fortieth year. I saw him today in his coffin. Perhaps fifteen of us remembered him enough to come, remembered through the twenty years he had been away. I have been away, too, but the coincidence doesn't mean much to any of them, about Simon and me. There's no reason it should. I had to come back anyway, for other reasons, and I had returned several days before he died. But there was no way for me to know it was going to happen.

So Simon has come back, and all of us wonder why his father brought him back to lie beside the mother he murdered.

But looking down into his quiet white face I knew that there would be no more specters to appear before his tortured eyes, no chimera in a white nightgown to convulse his puny brain into murderous aberration, no more ghosts for Simple Simon.

He had left them all to us.

***

Byron Hoot
Wexford, PA

Untamed Hope

I never tire looking at edges
Where woods and fields or
Yards meet.
          There what
Is untamed survives,
Lives, lets itself be seen
As the hope it is—
Close but never taken in.

Maxine Weintraub
Wayland, MA

Does Your Grandma Bake Cookies?

Things you might hear in a first grade class early in the school year. Somewhere in America.

"Today we are going to talk about our families. Let's start with grandmas. They are always fun to talk about. And let's talk about what they do for us. And what they make for us. We'll go around the room. Does your grandma bake cookies?"

"Ummmm, no. But my grandma taught me to play poker. She is something called a dealer in the West."

"My grandma is a cowboy on her own ranch. She taught me to ride a pony."

"Oh, no, my grandma cannot make cookies. She makes pizza in a pizza place in New York City. Good pizza."

"No. My grandma won't let me visit at her house. She runs a jail and she lives there."

"My grandma's name is Arlene and she has red hair with white on the top. She brings fancy cookies in a box. With ribbon."

"No, silly. My grandma works at night. She works in a big office building using mops and brooms. She sleeps all day."

"Yes. My grandma drives the school bus and eats cookies all day long. She is fat."

"My grandmother does not believe in cookies! She teaches yoga and has a dark belt in something. She has lots of muscles and eats green stuff."

Maxine Weintraub
Wayland, MA

"My grandma used to make cookies but my mother says now she has forgotten how."

"My grandma works for the country. My mother says she is a spy and we should never eat anything she makes because it might be poison!"

"My grandma is mayor of our town. She is too busy to make cookies but keeps chocolate kisses in her desk drawer just for me and my brother. My father says my grandma is a pain in the butt and wouldn't do anything for anyone including making cookies. I like her. She smells fancy."

"My grandma used to carry mail to people's houses. Now she is afraid of dogs and walks around carrying a spray gun. She does not eat cookies."

"My grammie does not make cookies. She carries little bottles around in her purse and drinks from them in the bathroom. She trips a lot."

"No. We don't see my grandma much. She drives a taxi cab in Chicago, I think."

"I don't know. She teaches school. Not here. Ohio."

"My grandma hides her cookies under the sofa and lies down all day watching murder on t.v."

"Yes, my grandma makes cookies. She also writes short stories and sends them to magazines. They send them back. 'What do they know?' she says."

Everyone in every class clapped and shouted YES when asked if they loved their grandmas. Even the spies and the prison wardens and the red head with white roots!

Amanda Noble
Miami, FL

In Her Nature

Ever changing,
She and I—
Attempts to balance
Our Facets,
Our World.
She is who she is,
At the core.
Yet, her surface is
Fragile with transition.
Some change her—
Ornamental make-up.
Others bring her down to Earth,
Only to build her up again.
Some leave her alone
And appreciate her growth.
Inspiring from afar.
Fascinating under the scope.
She is who she is.
Ever changing,
She and I.

Thomas Peter Bennett
Bradenton, FL

Terror on Departure

There was fear in her eyes
as the attendant escorted her
from the overbooked
coach-class section.

Her anxious tap-tapping
on her wooden cane
echoed her heavy breathing
that erupted into sobs.

She gripped her timeworn bag,
in a papery finger embrace and
twisted it, her knuckles white,
in terror and disappointment.

Through a veil of time,
I saw my future self in her.
I should have risen, offered
my seat, but I sat pat.

Minutes later she reentered,
attendant-escorted, to an
empty first-class seat.
Smooth flight ahead.

F. Anthony D'Alessandro
Celebration, FL

My New Team

I walked behind the groaning, lumbering man.
A head taller than my oversized refrigerator,
he leaned left like a ship hit on its port side by a torpedo,
listing and swallowing gallons of sea water.
He sensed my sliding steps,
looked back from behind a latticed and lacy face,
then clutched a nearby chair.
He gestured and waved me past him.
It struck me, much like a giant puck
crashing into a distracted hockey goalie's face.
I am one of them.
They are no longer them. Rather, they are me.
      They're on my team.
Another snowy headed man stutter stepped past me
      at the car dealership.
He excused himself, and I stepped aside
making sure I'd held the door for this seasoned one.
Strange, while calling me, "Sir," he stood at the door
      waiting for my exit.
Why? Was he really holding it open for me?
We were herded into the waiting room
while our wrench wielding mechanic pulled out his
repairman's stethoscope.
I was running out of patience for the drama
belching across the grainy, wall-blanketing TV screen.
I assessed the props and people surrounding my life stage.
A dozen devotees of the TV soaps slouched and watched
      droopy-eyed,
snored, or walked up in a procession queuing for
      free coffee.
A raucous snowy beard sparked a high pitched snoring
      concerto.

F. Anthony D'Alessandro
Celebration, FL

Others joined in, uninvited.
As I sympathized for that poor old timer and his band of
        fellow sleepers,
I felt gentle tapping on my shoulder.
A man in a blue work uniform said, "Sir, your car is ready.
        Sorry to wake you."
I looked up at the clock. How did those minutes escape
        from my day?

***

Sylvia Little-Sweat
Wingate, NC

Night Driving

The illumined gray highway
tows me along steep mountain
passes past laurel slicks that fill
dark crevasses, past feral eyes
that flash, stark and aware,
in a slash of fleeting light.
Night reclaims all valleys.
Ahead, still out of sight, a lynx
climbs a crag, crouches above
its prey while I shift to second
gear to swerve with the curves
that uncoil and disappear
into the night like fleeing
snakes. Transmogrified, I
cast a raptor eye, join all
that forage in the dark.

Robert Erickson
Round Pond, ME

My Grandfather's Oars

These are my grandfather's oars
Silently sending me on my course
The surgical slicing of the sea
Oh, what these oars mean to me

Dipping, dipping, guiding my way
Rekindling the love of another day
The oars he built are as thin as was he
When I row, it is like he is holding me

As I glide toward the distant shore
Each stroke closer to his door
Grandfather is with me wherever I go
All I need do is sit down and row

***

A Tree of Love

Carved softly on the tree of life
In words so gentle, crisp and clear
Words that say, "I love you dear"
Fashioned from a lover's knife

They lay beneath these lovely boughs
Fondly held in each other's arms
Feeling all of God's earthly charms
Carved forever these sacred vows

Arthur Kramer
New York, NY

Carpe Diem

"Carpe Diem": Two words occasionally adorning the transom of the many vessels we encountered; a simple, yet powerful reminder of the quintessence of life, and the raison d'etre for our voyage. Words that ring even more acute years later as we relive what now seems to be almost a fantasy, washed away like a footprint in the sand. Did we really do it, or did somebody else do it? Or were we somebody else when we did it? No matter—it is over, as sure as yesterday and the last nanosecond, but its aftershock lingers forever. Those two years will remain a beacon for many to come and, as life goes on, will be an inspiration for us to continue to seize the moments as they arrive. Armed with that ancient Phoenician proverb—*the gods do not deduct from man's alloted span, those years spent sailing*—and leaving a quarter of a century of teaching behind, my bride and I set sail, the day after our Lady of the Harbor's one hundredth birthday, to shores and seas unknown. An ocean crossing is not an unusual event in today's world, but for us, in our small ketch, it was the most remarkable event of our lives. For many dream, and many live these events vicariously, but we were making it a reality —a two year voyage to Europe and back via the Caribbean. Contrary to what images the media may conjure, sailing a small boat offshore can be downright uncomfortable. Why then, in this modern day when one can fly across the ocean in a few hours in safety and comfort, should we want to risk our lives and endure many hours of discomfort to sail a small boat across the sea?

The answer lies precisely in the alternative. In this present day we are led through almost every step of our lives: told what to wear, when to sleep, how to eat, when to go, when to stop, when to turn, how to cope with stress, doors open and close for us, moving walkways carry us up, down, and for-

Arthur Kramer
New York, NY

ward...., one's basic instincts are rarely put to the test. A small boat at sea offers a constant physical and mental challenge, a return to the essential nature of things, a chance to really know oneself and for some, better therapy then money can buy. If this were the only reason, however, I doubt that we would have had over two hundred boats sailing back with us from the Canaries to Barbados in December '87. They were also there for the magnificent sky with its myriad stars and superb sunsets, the ever changing primal sea with its schools of playful dolphins and cavorting whales, the sudden human closeness and camaraderie that might require years on land to nurture and those few exquisite moments of exhilarating sailing that, in itself, make it all worthwhile.

Our first passage of 22 days and 2200 nautical miles from New York to the Azores had more than its share of wonderful moments: endless sunny days under a soft following wind, moonrise on the bow bigger than life in the wee small hours of the watch, dozens of leaping dolphins playing tag with the bobstay, Portuguese men of war drifting beside us as we lay becalmed on a windless surreal sea, freshly baked bread delighting our sense of smell and taste, humpback whales performing that little understood ritual of flapping the sea with their fins.....and....its share of uncomfortable moments: a leaky exhaust system that had to be drained every day to prevent flooding of the engine, a stationary front with hurricane force winds and fifteen foot seas that we had to endure for 24 hours, a loose valve in the head that threatened to flood the bilge, our brave crew member Nancy constantly seasick and needing injections of compazine at times to control the nausea and vomiting, her strong-willed husband Milt, after too many days at sea, steering his own course rather than what the skipper wanted.

Horta, Faial, our landfall in the Azores was a special place. Lying in the middle of the Atlantic, far from the cruise ship lanes and tourist routes, it is a yachtie's paradise. Small boat sailors from almost every continent head there for R&R.

Arthur Kramer
New York, NY

A volcanic isle exploding with hydrangeas and filled with the beloved Azoreans who manned many of the U.S. whaling ships, begot a storybook atmosphere. They say you will always return to Faial. We are believers.

Narrowly missing some heavy weather, and blessed by good winds and following seas, we then swiftly sailed the remaining 1000 miles to the "Old World." Landfall at Cabo Sao Vincente, the southwestern most point of Europe, was a delicious moment, an inkling of how Cristoforo Columbo must have felt five hundred years ago when he thought he reached the East Indies.

We had crossed the "pond" (as it is affectionately referred to by small boat sailors), or more reverently put, God had afforded us a safe and "uneventful" (as the media would describe it) ocean passage.

The cruise then took on a different dimension as the boat transformed from a passagemaker into a floating home. For six mild winter months we lived in a marina in Estepona, Spain, a town on the Costa del Sol, which still retains much of its 19th century charm. We became captives of the spirit and romance of España, its people, its fiestas, its culture, its countryside, the wine, the music, the flamenco. The boat was our turtle shell home, giving us a foothold in a foreign land and a warm welcome from the people and the yachties alike. The ocean passage, a dream and desire for many years, surprisingly began to fade as the highlight of our journey. What became the richest and most lasting part of the experience were the strangers from another country who transformed into close personal friends overnight. This touched us deeper and made our days so very special.

Spring found us with that common marina malady: hull paralysis.We found it difficult to untie the lines. A complete transformation had occurred from ocean voyagers to dockside liveaboards. However, as the trek of the other boats began east we eventually cast off, shedding Spanish tears to our surprise, and closing a chapter in our life. The whole

Arthur Kramer
New York, NY

Mediterranean lie before us and we quickly discovered that a few in depth quality experiences were much more meaningful than many superficial ones. Our pace slowed down and our enjoyment increased as we cruised the southern Spanish coast, the Balearic Isles, Sardinia, Corsica, Sicily and the land of Homer: Ithaca and its Ionian neighbors. Though the days were filled with endless exploration of the cultural treasures, the towns, the markets, the harbors, the underwater life, the countryside, the restaurants, etc., people and personal contacts continued to penetrate us the most. Today there remain those special friendships that need only a phone call to rekindle, as if only days, not years, had passed.

As we sailed west through the straits of Gibraltar on that windy moonlit night in November '87, we knew we were leaving most of the best days behind. Not all of them though, as what lay before us were some of the best sailing ever with following seas and strong trade winds, a virtual "sleighride" home. The Mediterranean is not a paradise for sailors. It is a large enclosed basin ringed with mountains and many microclimates which continually spawn their own competing weather systems. Wind direction can change several times in the course of a day and dead calm can be quickly followed by gale force winds.

Many islands lie in our path back across the Atlantic from the Canaries to Barbados, Bequia, St Lucia, Martinique, Dominica, Guadeloupe, Antigua, St. Croix, St. John, Tortola, the Bahamas... sounds almost like many winter vacations rolled into one! Well, it differed by one unique ingredient: we never left home, which gave us a sense of belonging to each magic isle. We never quite felt like the one and two week tourists that surrounded us. We filled our days with unsurpassed sailing, snorkeling, beach barbecues, and occasional forays into the island interiors.

Sadly, we watched those precious days diminish as our home weaved northward. In Tortola, we bid a grand farewell to our Spanish and Australian cruising friends of the past

Arthur Kramer
New York, NY

eight months and departed on the final leg of our journey. Landfall in Fort Lauderdale was, to put it mildly, a culture jolt. After two years of a simple life, propelled by one of the most primitive forces, walking into a suburban supermarket was tantamount to entering a time warp.

If this brief description of our two year sojourn sounds a bit fanciful, it's because the years have faded the less fanciful parts—as they will do. I can only say that whatever are your most innermost dreams—seize the day and bring them closer to reality.

***

Sally Belenardo
Branford, CT

The Wall

In summertime we walked along
the wall and lingered where
thick honeysuckle covered it,
perfumed the starlit air.

No longer does the wall divide
the lane from rocky beach,
nor fragrance of the laden vines
the wind unbounded reach,

though memory's persistent root
still clings beside the sea,
rebuilds the wall and brings to life
the one who walked with me.

Anne Hammond
Woolwich, ME

Be There

The tall ship calls, "Be there, enjoy the law of the wind."

HMS Bounty sails swiftly in gentle seas and heavy weather.
The crew climbs 100-foot masts to hang the sail, reel the
        canvas in.
When the ship pitches and rolls, hang on,
"One hand for the sail, one hand for you," said mariners in
        the age of sail.

HMS Bounty, built to film *Mutiny on the Bounty,*
Is 1789 vintage with three masts, square sails in four
        courses;
Skysail, topsail, two main, a spanker over the stern,
Three jibs on the boom to catch every breath of wind.

The tall ship calls, "Be there, enjoy the law of the wind."

She sails the East Coast of America and the
        Caribbean Sea.
What would it be like to sit on the skysail yard,
Release canvas as the ship heeled on the ocean?
What would it be like to steer a ship careening on waves,
Moving with each turn of the wind?

To sail aboard her is magic, when the sky is blue and the
        sea sparkles.
What bliss to watch her draw wind and cruise.
In stormy weather, excitement grows; the crew hauls to at a
        moments notice.
When the rain pours down, one is extraordinarily alive.

The thing is to: *Be there, enjoy the law of the wind.*

Anne Hammond
Woolwich, ME

Except for the day *HMS Bounty* tried to sail around
Hurricane Sandy.
Off Cape Hatteras, wind 40 knots, waves 18 feet, she
          foundered.
Fifteen crew rescued, one unresponsive.
The captain was never found.

***

Janet Leahy
New Berlin, WI

Afternoon of the Faun

Moving out of the woods
she prances through fresh snow,
plows the white powder
with her nose,
kicks a spray of fluff
behind her.

The race is on,
round the frozen pond,
over the hillside,
lithe body suspended in flight.
Graceful as ballet dancers in Debussy's
Afternoon of the Faun.

Be careful dear, the city speeds
toward you in streaming lanes
of traffic.
You who bolt forward
never looking left or right—
wearing your lovely winter pelt.

Goose River Anthology, 2013//67

Elmae Passineau
Wausau, WI

The Third Child

The third child
(of whom not much is expected)
has to live up to big brother the pilot
(our son is smart enough to fly those big jets)
and big sister the nun
(our place in heaven is secured)

She'll never finish college
(all her friends went right to work earning money)
She'll never get another degree
(why spend all summer five hours from home?)
She'll never be a principal
(just teach and leave that to the men)
She'll never be a pilot
(why do something so dangerous?)
Her marriage won't last
(what do they have in common?)

Well, she did, she did,
      she was, she was,
      and it did.

Janet Morgan
Wiscasset, ME

Shotgun Shells

Mother's Day is one of those special days designed specifically to bring back fond remembrances. There are an abundance of memories that I could use to illustrate my mother's special qualities, but the most vivid is an example of her secret nature. Just when I thought I knew everything there was to know about her, she did something that shook me to the core. She was an even-tempered person, but on one occasion she not only lost it, but she showed my brother and me a flash of gutsy behavior. Eddie was six and I was eleven when we found out what she was cable of when fully aroused.

It was a crisp fall day—probably a Saturday, for my brother and I were home—when shots were fired very close to our home. Those shots were coming from behind the house on our eighty-plus acre property. As the booming continued, Eddie and I ducked under the dining room table while our mother dashed to the nearby window. It was hunting season, but no one hunted in our quiet residential neighborhood.

My father, the avid hunter, was at his hunting camp—complete with a duck pond. That is where he spent his fall days off from work at the local power company.

A grunt of what sounded like rage escaped Mom's lips when she dashed for the front door. Eddie and I crept out from under the table and peeked out the window. Our eyes barely showed above the windowsill, but yes, we could see a man out there and he was shooting *our pheasants!*

And just why did we have pheasants? Our dad belonged to a local rod and gun club and one year they got the brilliant idea that they should do something akin to the "catch and release" plan that fishermen use. This, however, was to be a raise, release, and shoot plan. So, in a weak moment, Dad

Janet Morgan
Wiscasset, ME

agreed to raise the baby pheasants that the club purchased. On our back forty, the club erected a giant pen with a wooden framework encased in chicken wire. The roof was ten to twelve feet off the ground so that when the pheasants were old enough to fly, they could not escape.

The pen was large enough for literally hundreds of growing pheasants. Every spring they arrived and every fall they were set free. Before they could become tame enough to trust humans, they were crated up and released at the old Bailey Farm on the shores of the Sheepscot River. The pheasants were given a few weeks to acclimate themselves to the wild Maine woods before hunting season began. Then a second grand scheme was devised: someone—I doubt very much that it was my father—had the bright idea that Dad should keep a few dozen of the grown pheasants and let them mate, thus saving them the cost of purchasing babies every spring.

So there they were, safely copulating and laying eggs in covered nests my father had built. Or so we thought. They were safe until hunting season arrived.

I vaguely recall Mom yelling something like, "Stay inside," as she hit the ground running. She ran across the lawn and the field that was the summer home to our vegetable gardens. She was yelling all the way, but we could not hear her from inside. We just knew that she was MAD. Mad with capital letters as her legs tried to keep up with her waving her arms. The hunter looked startled when Mom literally flew up to the man, her arms wind-milling furiously. With her spare five foot four inch frame, she had to look up at the very tall and burley figure with a shotgun. Her stance—hands on hips and her jaw jutting out—was much like a drill sergeant looking into the eyes of a raw recruit.

After a heated conversation, Mom turned towards the pen and pointed. She wasted no time crossing to the door and entering the pheasants' supposed sanctuary. She picked up one dead pheasant after another, muttering all the while. As my mother exited the pen, she held three dead birds in each

Janet Morgan
Wiscasset, ME

hand. She began waving dead birds like banners on a battle-field before she swung the door shut with her hip. Dropping the birds, she latched the door and looked around, undoubt-edly checking on the remaining pheasants. They had all retreated inside those small houses my father had construct-ed.

By this time Eddie and I had advanced outside to listen in on the action. After all, the shooting was over, at least the ones from the stranger's shotgun. My mother gave him a lac-ing down as the man stood amidst shotgun shells littering the ground. He tried to convince my mother that he had not seen the fence on which he had rested his shotgun. Poking it through the chicken wire of a structure easily twice the size of a basketball court, the man must have been an idiot to think my mother would believe his ridiculous story. As he tried to convince her to let him have the birds, Mom ordered him off the property.

She then spun around and stalked back towards the house with all six pheasants swaying in her hands. With each angry step, Mom muttered under her breath. All the while the pheasants' long necks bounced around near my mother's feet. The man finally walked away, dejection evident in every retreating step.

By this time we knew Mom had seen us, but we made our own hasty retreat back inside. The front door soon slammed behind Mom and there she stood just inside the door. Anger finely was etched on her beautiful face. She said nothing to us, just gave us the *look* as she headed for the kitchen. Eddie and I just stared, first at her, then at one another, and final-ly back at her. We said nothing as we followed her through the dining room and into the kitchen. Mom dropped the birds gently into the large enamel kitchen sink before turning to us and calmly stating, "Meal change: we're having pheasant tonight."

Franklin W. Marshall
Simsbury, CT

Notes from a Misanthrope's Journal

View now:
sea-changes with red tides
from Myrtle Beach to Biscayne Bay,
precipitating at their ebb on storm-disheveled sands
a zone of recrements: mephitic kills of fish;
the wizened shells of crabs; the egrets'
bodies in putrescence ripening
like cultures on the agar of the algae!

Crest after crest,
a surge of gridlock on Third Avenue,
with silver smudges of emissions spewed
from busses, vans, and limousines, from cycles,
trucks, and carts, from chimneys, stovepipes,
funnels, pyres, boilers, ranges, forges,
unfold the psyche-wringing
debits of propinquity: the blare, the bleat,
the hoot of horns; a flailing of the arms;
the hammering of fists against the hood of cars;
diffusions of the excrement-and-copulation tropes
from mouths of laureates turned common herd.

Mile after mile,
in orange frames the billboards for tobacco,
perfumes, skin cream, churches, bibles,
tissues, spas
define a highway's marge that wends across
the erstwhile pools, canals, the green stocked
islands in a clear-cut Carolina swamp,
and in the west, black clods spill from the
maws of monstrous shovels, where the tailings
of strip mining leave moraines as broad
as (later to be broken) planks of politics.

Goose River Anthology, 2013//72

Franklin W. Marshall
Simsbury, CT

Within a wildlife park,
a poacher consummates a dream of opulence
with barrows stacked with tusks,
but at the site of slaughter on the plain
tonalities transmute
from gray of living hide to white of bones.

Too late,
too late, reclamatory spurs!
Before too long a time will be
when mineral and land depletion is a fact.
With conscience lost to graft and bribery,
misprision, non-feasance, collusion, barratry,
the profiteers, the wasters of the countryside hurrah,
for look: at nature's death
the world's finale will, at least, be colorful.

If only
a plague would come, a pestilence
so virulent that overnight
the single beast that swaggers when it walks:
this feral, fell, in civil specimen
that wills itself, as though a will
were truth, immortal settlements,
would vanish like its traceless forebears'
names, leaving clear the Earth, as once it was
before the injuries began—
clear for redwoods' panoply to shelter
a vine-and-fern-rich understory;
clear for a stag to scratch its winter coat
in peace against a thorny shrub;
clear for an aquifer to burst in jets
of unenvenomed water;
clear for the gnats to shimmy up and down
the splinters shredded from a probe of light

(continued)

Franklin W. Marshall
Simsbury, CT

in passage through a forest's tracery;
clear for a sky to fix its blue estate—
a blue that will remain until the sun dies.

***

Liz Moser
Baltimore, MD and Phippsburg, ME

Enlightened

Still warm
a squirrel lay
in the center of the gray paved road

in perfect stillness,
paws clutched, eyes closed,
tail lax.

Never handle animals
who are sick or dying—
you'll get infected.

I picked him up

and felt softness,
richness in his shadowed fur,
moist heat of recent breath
between my fingers—he was so small.

I put him in the roadside grass;
he lies among the yellowed stalks
on sanded ground
where he'll decay unseen, slowly
melding with the earth.

Goose River Anthology, 2013//74

Gerry Rita Di Gesu
Union, NJ

Kevin

Nancy hesitated as we walked into church. "What's the matter, Mommy, you look sad."

"Oh, nothing, honey." I felt a lump in my stomach and wished this night was over. Christopher, 13, and my husband, Roger had found seats for us.

Parishioners were eager to participate in the Lenten Holy Thursday services. Members of the senior Catholic Youth Organization (CYO) would read a passage from the Bible, one for each Station of the Cross. Kevin's reading was the Twelfth Station—Christ dies. Socially immature and with few friends, Kevin had at last found a small niche within the CYO group and had invited family and friends to the service.

I was proud but upset that Kevin had volunteered. His childhood had been painful. A chronic asthmatic, he experienced serious learning disabilities which made school a trial for him. He was considered a klutz by peers who wouldn't include him in sports activities. A severe stutterer, he was labeled "retard" by classmates. Now fifteen and a junior in high school, he saw a speech therapist weekly as his speech still became unintelligible when he was nervous or upset.

But Kevin possessed a joy and zest for life. His wonderful optimism helped him cope with daily problems. We adopted Kevin at a week old, loved him like crazy and helped him in every way we could. But we didn't possess Kevin's inherent accepting and non-judgmental personality. He considered everyone a friend.

Monsignor greeted us, reminding us of what Christ had endured for us. All lights clicked off with only the light over the lectern glowing on the Bible. CYO members, dressed in white robes, shared their readings. Some were nervous and read so quickly it was hard to understand them while others, composed and confident, read slowly and deliberately.

Gerry Rita Di Gesu
Union, NJ

Finally, it was Kevin's turn.

He smiled as he opened the Bible to the passage he had practiced reading at home for many weeks. Chris and Nancy looked at me for reassurance I couldn't provide. "The...the...the..." Kevin began. His mouth twisted slowly as he tried painfully to say the next word. We sat paralyzed in the quiet stillness. He was "blocked"—unable to speak.

I tried not to cry. My family stared straight ahead, unable to look at each other. Then, as we waited in the soundless black church, I felt a tiny glow flicker inside of me. It grew slowly until I felt consumed by its radiance and realized it had to be the prayers of everyone in the church forming a single wave of hope directed toward Kevin, willing him to speak.

"Lord spoke." His mouth contorted painfully but finally he continued reading, halting for endless minutes between words. He took a deep breath from which he seemed to draw strength from all of us. A smile crept over his face as he continued reading the exceptionally long passage. He finished and stood there a moment, then grinned, gave a slight wave and stepped down from the lectern.

Nancy hugged me and I had to grab Chris' hands to stop him from applauding. The final passages were read. As the church lights clicked on, I felt as if I had been on a long journey and was returning to reality. My family sat silently, saying thank you in their own way.

I thought Kevin might be upset or embarrassed but should have known better. God's wonderful gift of optimism hadn't let him down. He stood in the center of a large group, grinning broadly.

"That was great, Kev. We felt Jesus' pain when you were trying to speak."

"Congratulations on a great job. You really hung in there. I would have flipped out."

"Boy you really have guts."

He laughed as CYO members gathered around—at last

Gerry Rita Di Gesu
Union, NJ

part of a group.

Father Charles, the CYO moderator, hugged Kevin tightly. "Kevin, you're our hero. I'm so proud of you. Everyone could imagine Jesus' agony and suffering as we watched you struggle. Your pain certainly showed how the Lord suffered before He died. You gave the word courage new meaning."

Finally, Kevin joined us. "Hey, Mom, I told you not to worry. I knew I could do it. At first I really got upset when I got stuck. But then I remembered what my speech therapist tells me: "Kev, when you have something to say and people care about you, they'll wait til you can finish. And isn't it great. She was right."

***

George Wentz
Sturgeon Bay, WI

Humility

Leaves, stay up in your tree;
Wind, don't blow cold in my face;
Sun, stay awhile longer each day;
Rain, fall softly only when needed.

Road, be easy on me through life;
Music, be kind to my ears;
Wine, age well with character;
Friend, be loyal and forgiving.

For these I would want
If I could have my way.
Alas, I have no control of them—
My hope, at least, is for a friend.

Meredith Fossel
Alna, ME

Bird Tree

A white pine, once a big one
with thick branches below
and rung upon rung of branches tapering up

in every season birds love this bare tree

arrange their bodies along its limbs
then fly up and settle down again
in different patterns

they call out their restless songs
push each other around
and make a big fuss when I go out
to take a picture of the tree
in the snow, against greening grass
framed by browns and golds
eleven years times four seasons
worth of pictures now

the tree was straight at first
each year the trunk leaned further
shoved and heaved by wind and frost
until one spring the bottom set of branches
touched the ground on the uphill side

next winter these broke off
and a second set rested on the hill
the angle grew more acute year after year
the set of branches holding it
moved further up the tree

the birds were fine with all of it

Goose River Anthology, 2013//78

Meredith Fossel
Alna, ME

last spring, in the Patriot's Day storm
the whole tree tumbled down
now the birds perch on the tips of branches
that reach straight up into the sky

***

Watching the Haying With Gigi

Malcolm, who uses our field for his cows—
keeps it limed and fertilized, sells the hay
and gives us a side of beef in exchange—
has started this year's haying.

I make time to watch it every year.
Gigi's seen the haying, too,
but now that she's three
she pays attention
and asks why at every step.

The tall ripe grass
is flattened in an afternoon
behind the cutter bar on the John Deere
with a red and white umbrella
duct-taped to the seat.

The tractor's back in the morning
pulling a spider-legged machine
for tedding—Gigi and I call it fluffing up—
to dry the hay
and in the afternoon
they rake it into windrows.

Goose River Anthology, 2013//79

Meredith Fossel
Alna, ME

On the third day Malcolm
attaches a baler to the tractor
with a hay wagon tethered behind—
takes most of the morning
to get it working right.

Finally the baler gathers,
binds,
and shoots
square bales
into the sky
where they seem to pause
before they plummet
into the hay wagon.

I see the joy of it in Gigi's face.

***

Sally Belenardo
Branford, CT

Clover

White clover-strewn lawns:
Earth has star fields of her own,
the daylight hours.

Robert B. Moreland
Pleasant Prairie, WI

Harbor House Residence,
Sunday Afternoon

Mother's Day and she cannot say
the simple "I love you" through
dementia's darkest fog. The stroke
has taken a little more away.

Does she remember the rocking chair,
content babe in her arms, suckling
at peace; innocent of the
outside world that waited?

She bandaged his knees, kissed
the "boo boos" to make them well;
salving esteem when he was broken
with milk and chocolate oatmeal cookies.

All his life he looked to his father,
approval unspoken. He would not.
She loved away the moments through
sun dappled summers with butterfly kisses.

So he strokes her wrinkled cheeks and
gazes into those deep blue green eyes
praying for a relief to her suffering
all the while whispering, "I love you, Mom."

Byron Hoot
Wexford, PA

Divine Distraction

I think I would know the sound
Of God's footstep in the woods
Distinct from deer or bear,
Turkey or squirrel, or chipmunks
Running across leaves.
                               Like some
Memory of a dream suddenly
Transposed into what is right in
From of me, I'd say, "Aha!
There it is . . ." my voice declining
Into whisper as I look to see
The invisible among the trees,
The stride a little longer than a man's,
A little louder than a deer's
When an echo turns my head
And as I look back
My eyes and ears are in argument
Because I did not see what I
Hear leaving quietly.

***

A Brief Essay on the Nature
of Things

Yes.
Thank you for
Your attention.

Goose River Anthology, 2013//82

Maureen Anaya
Berwick, ME

A Heavenly Meeting

The Amtrak train, between Portland and Boston, came to an abrupt stop at a small Maine town to pick up some passengers. As the train slowed down it suddenly came to a stop. Carl Perkins glanced out the train window and observed the passengers as some got off and others boarded the train. Then he saw a beautiful woman waiting for someone. Her shoulder length blonde hair glistened in the sunlight, as the unearthly glow in her dark green eyes was offset by a perfectly shaped oval face and lovely red lips. Her skin was lily white with a translucent glow. Her long white dress flowed in the breeze. The young woman watched intently as the passengers disembarked; however, whoever she was waiting for didn't arrive. She stood silently as the train picked up speed. Carl looked away for a minute, to secure his laptop, and then looked back. She disappeared from sight.

Carl returned to his small apartment in Wells, Maine. He couldn't get the image of the beautiful woman out of his mind. He turned on the TV and placed a ready-made meal in the microwave, popped open a can of beer and sat back to relax. He lived a solitary life, since he left behind a girlfriend and family in Upper New York State for a job opportunity, which happened to be in Portland, Maine. The accounting firm offered him a great salary and benefits. Since he graduated and became a certified public accountant it had been a struggle, in this job market, to find anything equivalent to the salary he needed to pay back his school loan.

Carl sat back in the chair until he heard the microwave bell ring. Dinner was ready so he proceeded to take the meal out and place it next to him, allowing it to cool off as he continued to watch TV.

Memories of home and his mother's home cooked meals came back to him. She was the backbone of the family, since

Maureen Anaya
Berwick, ME

his father was in ill health. Not only did she keep a tidy home, but worked outside the home as sales lady in a department store.

Carl was the middle child. He had an older sister and a younger brother. His medium build, sandy brown hair, and soft brown eyes made him look mediocre or perhaps it was his thick rim glasses; however, he excelled in every subject and made Judy's acquaintance in trigonometry class. They started dating but nothing serious developed. It was sad to say goodbye to everyone but he had to leave for financial reasons.

Carl rested comfortably in a chair and fell asleep. He dreamt of the beautiful lady he had seen at the train stop.

The next day he followed his daily routine, he caught the commuter train and opened his laptop to catch up on some work before he arrived at the office. He dutifully worked on some accounts trying to make points with his boss, Mr. Stevens, who considered him an excellent employee. There was an opportunity for advancement, since a couple of managers were going to retiring; however, for now he was content with the job he was assigned. The day was busy with clients filing yearly income taxes.

The ride home on the Amtrak was as usual; however, when they came to the small Maine town, the same lovely woman he had previous seen, was again waiting on the platform. The train pulled away with her standing there, only this time he could see her crying. This happened over the next few days and he wondered if anyone else noticed her.

Carl was so moved by this sad young woman that he requested a day off to find out more. *Did she need help?* He was going to get to the bottom of this mystery.

"Oh, tomorrow is Valentine's Day. You have special plans. Of course you can have the day off," Mr. Steven said.

It would be too weird to explain why he wanted the day off, so he went along with Mr. Steven's assumption.

The next day, Carl took the commuter train, as usual,

Maureen Anaya
Berwick, ME

but got off at the small Maine town. A couple of passengers were waiting to get on the train, but the young woman was nowhere in sight. The train pulled away from the station. Carl looked around, to see what the town had to offer, and wondered how he could find the beautiful woman. He viewed a coffee shop and decided to stop there and inquire. He ordered a coffee and started a conversation with the waitress who seemed a bit nervous when he inquired about the love-ly lady who waited for the Amtrak commuter train.

"Your best bet is to get information from Laurie who works at the flower shop." The waitress advised then seemed to avoid engaging in further conversation about the mysteri-ous lady.

A block down the cobble stone walkway was the flower shop. The name of the shop was LAURIE'S GARDEN. When he glanced, though the store window, he saw the woman whom he was seeking. She stood behind the sales counter ringing up orders. Her face was framed in a lovely bouquet of roses, which she was selling to a customer. The sight took his breathe away. He had to talk to her. Why was she wait-ing for the commuter train and someone to arrive? The cus-tomer, left the shop clutching the box of flowers as Carl entered.

"May I help you? We have a fresh shipment of roses," she said as she stepped towards him with a sample red rose. She was dressed in a pink pantsuit with a stylish white blouse.

He took the rose and looked into her deep green eyes. I hope you don't mind if I ask you a question. It's personal"

"No, go ahead," Laurie said.

"I see you every day at the Amtrak station as the com-muter train pulls up to the platform and whoever you are waiting for never arrives."

"It's not me but the spirit of my identical twin sister, Lucy. She alway waited for her love but one day he never came. Someone killed him in the city. She used to meet him every day as the Amtrak Commuter came through town. Her

Maureen Anaya
Berwick, ME

spirit still waits for him. She died of a broken heart," Laurie put her head down and tears rolled down her face.

"I didn't mean to upset you. Are you married or engaged to anyone? If not, I would like to take you to lunch," Carl stated.

"No, there are not too many eligible men in this small town," Laurie seemed to recover from the dark thoughts of her twin sister.

"I would like to purchase a dozen red roses for you," he offered.

A smile came over Laurie's face. "I would like that very much. I could close the shop for an hour."

Carl didn't know where he would hang out until noon, but he knew when he saw Laurie she was the one. He found a comfortable bench where he could sit and read a book on his kindle. Time passed and he returned to the flower shop, where Laurie was tiding up and ready for lunch.

The small town café was a quiet quaint place where they discuss intimate details of their lives and get better acquainted. Laurie explained that her and her twin sister Lucy grew up in this quiet town. Lucy was introverted but Laurie considered herself extroverted. They didn't discuss Lucy's sad ordeal but instead talked about the future. Carl found out Laurie's parents had passed away and she was all alone trying to get by financially with the flower shop, which she had purchased through her parents' life insurance.

They planned to see each other on the weekends.

When Carl took the Amtrak, next day, and it made a stop in the small Maine town, Lucy's spirit did not reappear. She seemed at rest.

A year later, on Valentine's Day, Carl and Laurie married and he moved to the small Maine town where Laurie had her flower shop. They named the first baby girl Lucy. It seems Lucy's spirit rested after her twin found true love.

To thank Lucy for getting them together, they left a dozen red roses on her grave every Valentine's Day.

Irene Zimmerman
Milwaukee, WI

Visiting a Friend With Alzheimer's

When the yolk of her mind broke in mid-life,
her two best friends came to visit, hoping
their sunny-side-up stories of fun together
would help to unscramble her brain.

Remember camping at Long Lake last fall?
Beth began with a nervous laugh. *Remember*
eating popcorn around the bonfire at midnight?
Nothing coagulated behind their friend's eyes.

I picked a bouquet of your favorite flowers,
Jane chimed in, offering a vase filled
with white and yellow daisies. The woman
stared, unsmiling, then color climbed her face.

Her forehead found old familiar furrows
as she searched the hardening mind,
once sharp enough to keep a CEO on schedule,
and dished up two words: *From . . . you?*

She knew them! For a minute.
Her face faded again. An aide appeared
with a tray of meds, hesitated when she saw them.
Come in, they begged her. *We were just leaving.*

They hugged the cracked shell of their friend,
promised to come again, and hurried out the door.
Who . . . those . . . people? they heard her ask,
the monosyllables spattering the walls behind them.

Goose River Anthology, 2013//87

Lilli Buck
Bristol, VA

The SS Man

The mother was kneeling in the village church.
Praying her rosary.
The censer swung, the choir sung
"All praise to you, Marie."

She heard a tumult in the streets.
She heard a hue and cry.
And through the stained glass windows she dimly saw
The troops go marching by.

The troops went marching by,
A-goose-stepping so high.
The SS men, all dressed in black,
Were doomed to do or die.

She went back to her home in the village,
Where she had an only son.
He was slender, tall, and handsome,
And he was so very young.

His hair was blonde, his eyes were blue,
And he had an eagle eye.
He stood in the doorway and he saw
The troops go marching by.

"Oh, Mother, that's what I want to do.
I want to join the SS men.
To be an elite trooper,
Our country to defend.

Lilli Buck
Bristol, VA

"I know I would look splendid
In that fine black uniform.
The girls would all admire me,
And follow me in a swarm.

"And I would be respected
Throughout the Reich and realm.
I want to serve the Fatherland
With Hitler at the helm."

"Oh, no, my son, now listen!
Don't you be an SS man.
For they will steal your soul from you.
Please try to understand.

"For if you are an SS man,
To Hitler you must swear.
And you must then do Hitler's bidding
Any time and anywhere.

"And if you swear to Hitler,
Then him you must obey.
He will lead you to damnation,
For our God he has betrayed.

"For 'Thou shalt worship the Lord thy God,'
And Him only shalt thou serve.
Oh, seek the path of righteousness,
And from the Lord's way never swerve.

"Your head is turned by big parades
And fancy uniforms,
And the ravings of a madman,
Who will make ten million mourn.

Lilli Buck
Bristol, VA

"Other lands have come to fear us,
And we will be despised,
For we are becoming pagans,
And villains in their eyes.

"That's not how I brought you up
On our little mountain farm,
To tend the flocks with gentleness,
And keep the lambs from harm.

"I brought you up in Mary's church
Beneath bell tower and steeple,
To serve the Lord with all your heart,
With simple, humble people.

"You want to be part of something grand,
For you're a callow boy.
But if you follow that wicked man,
Your soul he will destroy."

"Mother, don't you love our Fuhrer?
And can't you plainly see,
He has brought us from our dark defeat
To the brink of victory?

"He is our country's Savior.
We are an empire once again.
Where he leads me I will follow,
Anywhere and any when."

So Heinrich joined the SS men
Despite his mother's plea.
He wore a fine black uniform
With boots up to his knee.

Lilli Buck
Bristol, VA

And in his fine black uniform
He felt so very proud.
The ladies all admired him
And he stood out in a crowd.

They sent him not to the Western front,
To fight the Allied soldiers.
They sent him not to the Eastern front,
Where the snow blew ever colder.

They sent him into Poland,
To a concentration camp,
To send small children to their death
In chambers dank and damp.

"This is not the work of heroes,
As is proper for a man,
To fight a foreign army,
To defend his native land.

"This is the work of cowards.
Sending children to their death,
To strangle them with poison gas,
Which steals their life and breath."

He watched them grow weaker day by day.
He saw them starve and die.
He saw their hollow faces,
He looked into their pleading eyes.

He sent them to the gas chambers.
He heard their mothers cry.

Lilli Buck
Bristol, VA

Heinrich went back to his barracks
And lay down on his bed.
His heart, for so long hardened,
Was breaking now instead.

The still, small voice of conscience,
Which had whispered long in vain,
Was shouting like the thunder.
His tears fell like the rain.

He thought about the village church
Where he used to kneel and pray.
He thought how he was an altar boy
Back in his childhood days.

He thought about, "Thou shalt not kill,"
In Deuteronomy.
He recalled, "Blessed are the merciful,
For they shall obtain mercy."

He cried, "My God, what have I done?
I've lived a life of sin!
How many people have I killed?
It breaks my heart within!

"Too late to seek salvation,
It's too late to repent.
Too late to seek forgiveness.
All my chances have been spent.

"I should have listened to Mama,
For I have lost my soul,
And I must stay forever
In hell, while ages roll.

Lilli Buck
Bristol, VA

"For now I am an SS man,
And I cannot get out,
And I must spend eternity,
Where demons shriek and shout.

"The Americans are coming,
They will see what we have done,
And they'll hold us accountable,
After their side has won.

"I don't want my dear old mother
To ever find out or know
What happened to her altar boy
Whose soul was pure as snow."

***

Maude Olsen
South Bristol, ME

A Picture Already Painted

The river's wearing stripes this morning;
As if to follow suit, a line of gulls,
In perfect spacing, flies
Silhouetted in white
Against the dark green spruce.
The hazy air is still;
Not a ripple disrupts the somber bands of blue,
Nor breeze to prompt the trees to wave.

Hush! Old March is leaving soon,
And nature beckons April to the door.
We are all too ready to receive her
And bid farewell to winter yet once more.

Goose River Anthology, 2013//93

Patrick T. Randolph
Kalamazoo, MI

February Songs: Bringing Home Our Home

This afternoon, with skin awakening
Winds, my wife and I found our home—at last!
In the cradle of our smile, in the song
Of our eyes, in the shelter of our ears
Sang the sweet cry of our newborn daughter.

With her eyes closed and our grins open wide,
We conversed in the winter evening light:
We forgot to eat; we forgot to drink,
But in the cries and silence of Aylene's
Presence, we had finally found our home.

Parenthood would have to wait, for this was
And now is the birth of one amazing
Falling in love with Euphoria's wink;
The parent-child friendship beyond Time—
The home of our quiet grin's grinning light!

***

Carp Pond

Moon sonnets—

        iambic

                verse on ripples.

N. S. (Vish) Vishwanath
Shrewsbury, MA

The Tea Party

July 4th 1947: Madison, Wisconsin.
Twenty-seven-year-old Sheraz listened to senatorial candidate Joseph McCarthy deliver a fiery admonishment to the young and liberal audience at the University of Wisconsin to be wary of enemies from within. The fireworks that followed were spectacular.

Sheraz's thoughts those days were far away in his native India where someone had slit a nation's throat, unleashing rivers of blood. Partition, they called it. There would be two nations now, India and Pakistan, where one had stood since time began. "Freedom," the newspaper headlines proclaimed, omitting the prophetic qualifying clause "... but only from British rule."

A pensive Sheraz sat by the lake, his girlfriend Rosemary by his side.

"Do you think your parents will stay in India?" Rosemary's question captured a conundrum facing Muslim families across the Indian subcontinent—do they stay put or move to where *their kind* was in the majority?

Rosemary, a freshman, just nineteen, had not met a foreigner till she had bumped into Sheraz in the cafeteria. Tall, courteous, self-assured, Sheraz reminded her of James Stewart. She had fallen in love with him, much to the discomfort of her Lutheran parents. But love, it doesn't ask for a dossier before it strikes.

"Can't tell yet," Sheraz replied, "it will not be an easy decision for them. My grandparents and uncles and aunts have already moved to Peshawar."

Sheraz was born to a Hindu mother and a Muslim father. His parents had met at a freedom-fighters conference in Bombay where a nationalist named Gandhi was talking about respect, even for one's enemy, as an ideal to live and

N. S. (Vish) Vishwanath
Shrewsbury, MA

die for. At home, Sheraz was taught to respect all faiths. Early in life, Sheraz was taunted as a "mixed breed"—at school, on the playground, in his nightmares. He could have fought back, but didn't. *Discretion is the better part of valor, pick your battles wisely,* his mother had taught him.

On the day of India's independence from British rule, August 15th 1947, Sheraz's parents mailed a postcard. "Dear Sheraz," their succinct message said, "so many have sacrificed so much for this day. We have decided to stay in India. What are your plans?"

It took four more years for Sheraz to come up with a response. By then he had become "Dr. Sheraz Raza," a bright star in the theoretical physics cosmos. The nation builders back in India took notice. The Prime Minister of India personally wrote to Sheraz after having heard of his technical accomplishments and of his student-volunteer role in the freedom movement of the early 1940s. "Come back, son, let us rebuild this great nation," the handwritten letter said. Sheraz's roommate, Dr. Sharma, a distinguished scientist in the study of medicinal plants, had received a similar letter.

"Do you think we can make a difference?" Dr. Sharma wondered aloud.

"We must, Sharma. The motherland beckons. We owe her."

They turned down lucrative offers in corporate America to accept leadership positions at research laboratories in India.

That summer, Sheraz and Rosemary were married on her parents' farm near La Crosse. Sheraz wrote to his parents. "Dear Abba and Ammi—I am coming back to India, with your daughter-in-law." The family's reaction was mixed. Having to deal with a white Christian daughter-in-law was disconcerting.

After their move back to India, Rosemary took the town by storm with her Donna Reed looks and captivating manners. Sunday evenings were set aside for her and Sheraz to walk in the park. Then, Sheraz would relax alone in his den

N. S. (Vish) Vishwanath
Shrewsbury, MA

and write a diary.

Decades rolled by. Life unfolded in its many bearings. Sheraz's diaries, over fifty of them, found their way into various shelves in his study.

Present Day: India.
The visitor rang the doorbell next to a simple brass nameplate with the name "Dr. and Mrs. Sheraz Raza."

Dr. Raza went up to the door to greet the visitor. A monsoon downpour arrived moments later.

"Welcome. It is so nice of you to come. I hope it was not difficult to find this place. The roads have become such a mess, thanks to crooked contractors buying up polluted politicians."

"It's my pleasure, Dr. Raza. I'm looking forward to our discussion."

They made their way to a back porch overlooking a picturesque garden, roses on one side and aromatic herbs on the other.

"Beautiful roses," the visitor observed.

"Thank you. Rosemary raised them. I am sorry you will not get to meet her. She is visiting our daughter in Wisconsin. I'll be joining her in a few weeks."

The visitor hadn't heard of Dr. Raza till a week ago when a common friend had introduced them. Charmed by Dr. Raza, he had agreed to review Dr. Raza's manuscript which turned out to be an autobiographical rant, a tell-all tome aimed at embarrassing many prominent people.

"So, young man, did you get time to read it?"

"Yes, Dr. Raza. I have, and I am so flattered you have asked me for an opinion."

"And ...?"

"I have one overriding question, Dr. Raza," and inching closer, he added, "why the urge for this exposé now, sir, at this stage of life?"

Dr. Raza smiled. For almost two hours he rambled on

N. S. (Vish) Vishwanath
Shrewsbury, MA

and on, ricocheting from one subject to another, often losing his bearings in the foggy labyrinths of his memory. His discourse ended with, "So, am I supposed to just let these rascals go scot free? Aren't they accountable for what they've done to this country?"

The maid interrupted before the visitor could respond. Dinner was served. The monsoon rain continued. Flashes of lightning kept interrupting the dinner-table talk. Eventually the lights went out, plunging the room into darkness. The maid hurriedly went about lighting candles in the kitchen and the dining room.

"Looks like it will rain all night," Dr. Raza observed. "I wouldn't recommend public transportation in rain. Why don't you stay overnight? We'll make arrangements for you in the study. After breakfast my driver can drop you at your hotel."

"Thank you, sir. Sounds like a splendid idea. We can wrap up our discussion in the morning."

After dinner, Dr. Raza led the visitor into the study where the maid had lit several candles. On the divan were some pillows and a bed sheet. The candlelight, the scent of melting wax, the stuffy odor from the books, and the smoke from the mosquito repellant coil gave the cramped study a somber feel.

"Do browse through the books if you can read in this light. I have a good collection."

The visitor walked around the room. The bookshelves were stacked with books in a smorgasbord of languages, authors, subjects, and vintage. Some had not been touched in a long time. In one of the shelves was a stack of diaries, each about a centimeter thick, arranged chronologically, 1953... 1954....The visitor picked up one labeled "Dr. Sheraz Raza—1954." He scanned a page that he'd opened at random.

August 27, 1955: Rosemary is looking as pretty as ever. We went to see 'The Far Country' at the Metro. Scenes of the

N. S. (Vish) Vishwanath
Shrewsbury, MA

American West made Rose homesick. Interesting line in the movie, 'I don't need other people. I don't need help. I can take care of me.' Wrong. Everyone needs someone. I wish Abba and Ammi would accept Rosemary. They never visit. Communal riots broke out again in a nearby village. Lives were destroyed fighting over which nonexistent god was superior. Sad! Are we squandering our independence?

"Wow. Dr. Raza. This is certainly interesting," the visitor noted. "Is this the same angry Dr. Raza I was with before dinner?"

Dr. Raza chuckled. "Go ahead. Feel free to read the diaries. Who knows what gems you might find within?"

Then, he called for the maid to walk him to his room. "I'm afraid I must call it a night now. At my age I'm no longer a night person. We have water and cookies on the table in case you get the munchies. We'll meet again in the morning."

Alone in the study, the visitor took out a stack of Dr. Raza's diaries and began reading them in sequence. It was like playing with a flip book. The progression from page to page was hardly noticeable, but when he flicked thru them rapidly, a cinema of sorts came to life.

February 18, 1953: I like this town. Nice climate, pretty parks, mellow people. I took charge of the institute last week.

May 20, 1953: I smell rats. One had been running a loan-sharking racket under my predecessor's nose. He'd borrow money interest free from senior scientists and lend it to the gardeners and janitors at exorbitant interest. Yet another fellow has been telling my staff they are doomed because 'a muslim has taken over.' It's not easy to fire rats in government service.

December 27, 1956: We got the President's Award for Excellence in Science Research. I am a celebrity. Abba and Ammi have written from Peshawar. They will stay in Pakistan from now on. A Pakistani connection isn't good for my career. We'll just tell people they live in Bombay. See, Ammi, I still pick my battles wisely. Rosemary looks radiant. The baby is due in

N. S. (Vish) Vishwanath
Shrewsbury, MA

May.

May 10, 1957: Shirin arrived. Blonde hair, green eyes like her mother. Shirin means 'sweet.' I lit up a cigar, informed both sets of grandparents. My parents in Pakistan ask if we will raise her to be Christian or Muslim. What irony! She'll be raised to be fair-minded human, dammit.

May 29, 1964: Now, civil service bureaucrats lecture me about my research priorities. Corruption has infected all aspects of public and private life. It has come to my attention that a system of bribery is prevalent even to get an appointment to see me in my office. I am getting fed up. Shirin is just seven and speaks three languages. Rosemary sent me a postcard from Wisconsin saying Shirin likes to be on the farm. The plight of farms and farmers in our country is pathetic. I wonder what kind of India Shirin will find when she grows up.

May 20, 1971: Communal riots again. The best minds are leaving the country. Will Shirin have to follow? Is this the anarchical freedom we fought for?

December 10, 1971: I attended the conference of national research laboratory directors. It was nice to see Dr. Sharma again. His research on medicinal plants is going well. He is as brilliant and eccentric as I remember him. He gave me a document about an herb he has discovered. A few drops adds flavor to your drink. About twelve hours later, without leaving a trace, it slows down the heart and gradually stops it. Oh, that Sharma and his Shakespearean fascination for the macabre.

February 10, 1972: Abba and Ammi passed away in Peshawar last week. Abba died first. He was 82. Ammi died the day after. She was 73. They had marched with Gandhi during the freedom movement. How disgusted they must have been with the state of affairs in India and Pakistan—two nations stuck in a messy morass. Rosemary, Shirin, and I grieved privately.

May 16, 1974: Shirin turned 17. We've decided to send Shirin to Wisconsin to live with her grandparents. She will go to college there. Here, colleges are charging bribes to admit

N. S. (Vish) Vishwanath
Shrewsbury, MA

meritorious students. We are doomed.

June 7, 1978: Rosemary turned fifty. Shirin graduated from the University of Wisconsin with a major in Agricultural Engineering. She wants to be a farmer. We are so proud of her. Her India days appear to be over. C'est la vie.

August 15, 1979: A letter from Pakistan arrived via registered post at the Institute. It was addressed to me. My next-in-command signed for the letter and promptly told a rat about his discovery of my 'Pakistani connection.' The rat called a powerful rodent in the corridors of power in Delhi. I received an urgent telegram: 'This is most serious STOP Request you immediately report to Delhi Headquarters STOP.' The contents of the registered letter have not been revealed to me yet.

January 30, 1981: Shirin is getting married in June. Her fiancé is from Green Bay. Good looking boy. We are assured pretty grandchildren. We are looking forward to the wedding in June. Eighteen months have passed. I have been made a lame duck while they investigate my non-existent Pakistani connections.

May 13, 1981: The worst months of my life got worse. Last week, the Central Bureau of Investigation notified us of our passports being impounded. We'll not be able to attend the wedding. Shirin is heartbroken. So is Rosemary. She saw me cry for the first time. God, please stay with me through my ordeal.

July, 4th 1982: Relief. I have been unconditionally exonerated. The letter that started all of this has disappeared. I wonder what it said. I prevailed. My enemies are neutralized. It was magnanimous of the Prime Minister and other luminaries to intervene on my behalf. The rodent in Delhi and the rat in my office have been dismissed, but have found lucrative positions in the private sector. My next-in-command had a role to play in my troubles, but didn't get punished. I have decided to retire. I will hunt them down. There is no joy in walking the halls of science anymore. I will focus on consumer activism, still in its infancy here.

N. S. (Vish) Vishwanath
Shrewsbury, MA

April 12, 1983—'Gandhi' won the most Oscars this year. Here, in India, you will soon be forgotten, Mr. G. The fox now guards the hen house. The rascals are winning.

October 17, 1993—Rosemary and I are in Wisconsin enjoying our grandchildren. Donna is eight. Jimmy is four. Cute as can be. We tell them stories of India's freedom struggle and of America's War of Independence.

July 2, 1997: The press has labeled me 'the godfather of small town consumer activism.' Some refer to me as 'a cranky version of Ralph Nader.' The corrupt police commissioner, the bribe-taking dean, the crooked public works contractor, the smooth-talking real estate scammers—our very own 'enemies from within'—are winning, when they should be hanging. James Stewart died today.

January 16, 2000: My activist life is not to Rosemary's liking. 'I can't handle this any longer,' she admonishes me. 'Stop tilting at windmills, Mr. Quixote. Get rid of your demons, write your memoirs or something, get a life,' she prods incessantly. Maybe she's right.

December 25, 2000: We moved to Tranquiliti Gardens outside the big city. Nice and quiet. Activism is mired in the bogs of political rascality. I'm too old for this. I opt out. Rosemary has partitioned the garden into 'his' and 'hers.' I now have an herb garden even Dr. Sharma would be proud of. The memoir is coming along well.

At this point the entries became less frequent and progressively more acerbic. The visitor got weary of reading about Dr. Raza's battles with the forces of evil. He blew out the candles and fell asleep to the sound of falling rain.

In the morning, Dr. Raza joined the visitor for breakfast on the porch, after which they strolled in the garden.

"Our country was once pristine like this garden till the rascals ..."

"Dr. Raza, with all due respect, sir, I must interrupt. I spent most of the night reading your diaries. What a remarkable life. I can appreciate your anger, your frustration at the

N. S. (Vish) Vishwanath
Shrewsbury, MA

way things are. Yet, I must leave you with one simple advice," the visitor paused. His tone became serious.

"Kill your demons, Dr. Raza. Let go."

"I was hoping the book would accomplish that."

"No, sir, it doesn't. It just gives them fresh life. Don't proceed with the book, sir."

Dr. Raza walked the visitor to the car.

"Thank you for coming, young man. I'll think about your advice. Maybe it's time."

"That's all I ask of you, sir."

After exchanging parting pleasantries, the visitor left.

A few weeks later, Dr. Raza called for his personal stenographer. He dictated a letter to be typed on his letterhead on high-quality stationery.

Sir,

We have known each other a long time. While I have been a source of much torment to you, please understand that my actions were motivated by my undying love for our nation. I am old now. It's time for peace. It's time for closure.

I would like to have the pleasure of your company on July 2nd at 5pm for high tea. It will give me an opportunity to do what I should have done a long time ago.

I hope you will graciously grant an old man his wish.

I look forward to seeing you.

Dr. Raza gave instructions to courier the invitations to half a dozen of his A-list demons.

July 2nd turned out to be a gorgeous day. Dr. Raza was a charming host. All the invitees came. Considerate of Dr. Raza's advanced age, they showed their tireless adversary utmost respect. It was a most peaceful evening. Apologies were made. Hands were shaken. The maid served a variety of sumptuous snacks. Dr. Raza personally went around serv-

N. S. (Vish) Vishwanath
Shrewsbury, MA

ing a thirst-quenching mango drink garnished with aromatic petals from his herb garden.

As the evening wound down, Dr. Raza raised a toast, "Gentlemen, I thank you for coming. God bless you."

The evening was a success by all counts.

That evening, before leaving for the airport, Dr. Raza couriered a package addressed to Dr. Sharma. Inside, a note said: "Thanks for lending this to me, old friend. It was most useful. Sorry about holding on to it for so long."

The flight to Wisconsin was smooth.

July 4th: La Crosse, Wisconsin.

The grandchildren gathered around Rosemary and Sheraz on the banks of the Mississippi, waiting for the fireworks display to begin. Sheraz lit a cigar and leaned over to kiss Rosemary.

"Sweetheart, I finally did what you've been asking me to do. I got rid of my demons. I killed them all."

The fireworks that followed were spectacular.

***

Patrick T. Randolph
Kalamazoo, MI

Alleyway Café

Small breakfast—

        He hungers

            for company.

P. C. Moorehead
North Lake, WI

Green Comes

Green comes, blowing through a forest of yeses,
renewing the earth,
renewing me—
a forest of yes and yes and yes,
each tree adding its voice—
a forest,
yes!

***

Breath

The forest is green and green and green.
Tall trees inhale,
and I, short that I am,
breathe.

***

Short

The grass is short.
Green moss shows.
I am growing.
Life is living.

Anne Hammond
Woolwich, ME

Killer

A bald eagle chases two turkeys in the meadow.
Turkeys take off, wing to the edge of the woods.
A marsh hawk swings down on a mouse,
Leaves wing prints and a body shape in the snow.

It happens every day in the field, in the bay,
One animal after another, one bird after another.

A coyote after a turkey, a fox after a crow.
Shore birds on the marsh, heron, egret
Follow the rills for fish once the wormer has passed.
Striped bass enter for the shiners in the waters.

Life is offered for sacrifice.
Life is taken by a predator,
Creatures circling every field, every air space,
Every spot of soil, every wood lot.

Where are you on the scale of life?
To whom do you offer your body?
The grizzly bear on Brooks Range, North Slope Alaska?
The wolves in Minnesota Lake Country?

The hunters of Iran, Afghanistan, Algeria?
Which one do you wait for?

Elmae Passineau
Wausau, WI

Dragging the Dress Across the Floor

Peeled from sweaty skin,
Hair becoming undone,
Home from the ball,
Yearning for sleep.
Prince Charming gone home across town
Wrinkled, weary, and sweaty, too.

Begun in glamour and glitter and glory—
swaying and swinging,
a blur of color, satin, and ribbon,
rhythm and sound intertwine...
Fabric wilting,
Flowers drooping,
Laughter and music diminish to silence.

Good night, good night,
Shoes shed, bag tossed, coat dropped—
up the stairs,
unzipping with each step,
down the hall,
open the door,
dragging the dress across the floor...

Steve Harvey
Biddeford, ME

Speaking to the Alien

You must understand our day
Hours here or there pounding or pretending to pound out
 things of consequence.
Things that rumble civilization forward crushing the
 civilized.
There is no time for excess; what time is not taken, is
 squandered.
Do what is expedient today and expendable tomorrow.

The cynic is the prophet. Conspiracy the motive.
Truth has not died, it is just ignored or forgotten or
 circumvented.
Or worst, just inconveniently left in the upper right hand
 dresser drawer
Beside the unused handkerchiefs.

Carpet tile is glued to wood floors and cannot be rolled
 back
And modular cubicles cannot be stacked in the corner so
 we can dance.
We rush to the next scheduled event and there is no sound
 of a tin can
Bounding across the brick pavement followed by shrieks
 and giggles of seven year old children.

Food is raised to be shipped and not eaten
Restaurant food is "fast" not savored;
Children and adults are entertained and cannot play;
The lack of attention is a disease
Not a sign that what we have civilized is not civilization.

Steve Harvey
Biddeford, ME

So when the day is over do not think me alien for the
      moment I take
To sit in front of the worn wheel parked on crumbling
      asphalt
And look across the chaos of colors creating disorder in my
      garden or
Kneel in the dirt, staining my pressed pants, to lift a flower
      seeing the sun's reflection.

***

Sharon Auberle
Sister Bay, WI

Comfort Me With Apples
for Emma Toft

Early September afternoon...the light is saffron, air like
      wine.
Bees hum their way through goldenrod and windfall apples.
Where Miss Emma's house once stood, Queen Anne's Lace
      and
chicory thrive. The barn remains, refuge for small animals.
I imagine she would want it so. Miss Emma's trees come
      and
go, the long bones of fallen ones turning softly into earth.
Her beloved lake recedes and rises, only its stony coast
      unchanging.
The days begin to shorten now. Soon enough, winter will
      come.

on the shore
a fishing pole
forgotten

Idella Anacker
Portage, WI

The Dwelling

An ordinary structure
      not unusual, surely not impressive
Oh, to be sure it had hosted birth—and death
      and every stage of life between
And it had served as a haven
      against seasonal storms and broken hearts
Joyously it had welcomed, then gave to the world
      three children
Surely other structures could boast the same
      and more
Why then such melancholy thoughts for old wood
      and bay windows
No reason, but for one
      It was mine.

***

Under Advisement

"Grandma, when we aren't here are you lonely?"
      he wondered with a frown.
"Yes." I answered softly
"Grandma, when we aren't here are you sad?"
      his little mouth turned down.
"Yes," I answered softly.
"Grandma, maybe we should stay here always."

"Honey, let me t.h.i.n.k about it,"
      I answered softly.

Joan Kotz
Portland, ME

Shadows of War

The chugging 2:38 steams into sight, whistles its approach, and with a screech of metal on metal, slows for its scheduled stop at the station. Canvas sacks stenciled "U.S. MAIL" are thrown out and thud, dead weight on the platform. At the open door of the passenger car, a rugged man with a duffle bag at his feet hangs onto the handgrip and strains for a glimpse of the town. As the train wheezes to a stop, he tosses out his bag, hesitates, and then steps down. He stands alone, looks up at the words "HAMPTON, MAINE" on the sign mounted near the peak of the roof, then gazes up Main Street. No one is there to meet him.

Roy Tibbetts takes up his bag, squares his shoulders and heads into town. Not much has changed: women doing their marketing on the shop-lined street, horse-pulled delivery wagons rattling by, and dogs barking when a Model T breaks the afternoon calm. Next door to the blacksmith shop, a gleaming gas pump now stands in front of the general store, and a handful of overalled men are gathered out front taking a moment in the sunshine to enjoy the year's first hint of spring. In the iron-fenced cemetery next to the white-steepled church, he notices rectangles of freshly disturbed earth. He walks on. No one seems to recognize or take notice of him.

Two years ago, young Tibbetts packed a few belongings and hitched a ride to war. Most of the other boys in town, handsome in new uniforms and itching to be doughboys, proudly marched away to fight "The War to End All Wars." Bands played, and the town turned out to cheer. Girls cried, mothers hugged and wept, and fathers lovingly and meaningfully patted slim backs and gulped back proud tears as their sons marched away eager to face the dangers and glories of war.

Joan Kotz
Portland, ME

Roy Tibbetts, though, left without fanfare. He considered himself to be a pacifist, a conscientious objector, and hoped to be able to sit out the conflict by staying home doing necessary work on the farm. But many in town called him a coward, and even his father seemed ashamed, so he looked for his own way to serve. Only his mother was there to wave good-bye when he hopped on the back of the neighbor's wagon and disappeared down the lane. Two months later, he was in France, a member of the newly formed American Ambulance Corps.

Fear, horror, danger, and sometimes boredom followed. He was assigned one of the new Ford ambulances nicknamed the "Tin Lizzie." In the open driver's seat, he drove through rain and snow, and he drove under the warm sun through devastated villages and across the furrowed but barren fields of France. He saw war: cowardice, savagery and extraordinary bravery. He carried stretchers in the trenches and saw death and dismemberment and the effects of dysentery and mustard gas on once strong young men. He saw things that he would never speak of for the rest of his long life. And, he saved lives.

Now he's almost home, disgusted by war but still proud of his service. His hometown looks about the same, but he feels like a stranger here. *How much*, he wonders, *has this abominable war changed him? Has his father forgiven him? Will his mother and sisters welcome him home?*

No one offers him a ride. He buttons up his olive-brown wool jacket, turns up the collar, and reties his boots. He shoulders his bag and his memories and starts the walk home. It's March, early spring in Maine, and piles of dirty snow edge the slushy street. He walks until he leaves the town behind. When he reaches the end of the paving he continues on the rutted dirt road. The narrowing way is still muddy in places and sometimes icy, but where the sun peeks through the tall trees, patches of sunlight dapple the road. The peaceful rustling of the woods and the sound of his

Joan Kotz
Portland, ME

own boots are all he hears, and the scent he's longed for the whole time he's been away but had lost the ability to recall now overwhelms him. How could he ever have forgotten the woodsy perfume of pine trees and their carpet of spring-damp, brown needles?

The bag over his shoulder grows heavier. His booted steps slow and almost stop in front of Helen's house, but her letters stopped coming after the first few months he'd been gone. He continues on down the lane. He's closer now to the farm, the old life, the chores, and the family. Two years. He was a boy when he left. He sees the picket fence ahead, and the elm trees in the yard, and his sisters' swing hanging from the sugar maple. As he opens the gate, a blur of black streaks out from the barn.

"Shadow?"

His duffle bag drops, and then his arms are full of wiggling, licking dog.

***

Thomas Peter Bennett
Bradenton, FL

Sunny Ice Man

A hard freeze last night
left powdered ice on the dock.
Under a cerulean morning sky,
we scraped and molded
slivers of ice to form a
miniature ice man.
He had fiddler crab arms,
sand grains for eyes, and
a mangrove seed for a nose.
His hat was a jaunty oyster shell.

Karen Lewis Foley
Topsham, ME

Listening to Bach on His Birthday

Glory, Glory in ribbons of sound
braided and layered in replications.
Continuo notes slide mellow
as butterscotch—recorders sigh—
strings swoop, leap high.

Glory glistens up down around—
then syllables punch
Germanic shouts
then descend to blend in chorale.

In his time Johann Sebastian
was considered old-fashioned,
Glenn Miller in the disco eighties.
But his sons who outshone him then
have faded to paler renown.

We lay down our work and bask
in the intertwine of fugue
lines caressing each other,
the double helix encoded in our brains
transmitting yet through generations, Glory, Glory.

**Charles Boldreghini
Collierville, TN**

A Father's Devotion

Many, many years ago when I was a little boy tagging along after my Grandmother Gatti, our day together began with me watching as she combed her waist length dark grey hair. And while she combed, her eyes would fill with tears and overflow down her cheeks.

When I was two, I thought she cried because the comb pulled at her hair and hurt. But by the time I was five, I had come to think there was some other cause for the tears. So, one morning after she'd pinned up her hair into a bun and was drying her tear streaked face, I asked her about it.

"Why do you cry when you comb your hair, Nonna? Does it hurt?"

She smiled and took my hand and led me to the kitchen table. She motioned for me to sit, and sat down beside me. For a moment she was silent, looking out the kitchen window. Then she turned toward me and began.

"One winter when I was twenty and living in northern Italy with my parents, I became very sick. I was burning with fever. All my hair had fallen out. The doctor who was caring for me told Papa he'd done all he could for me. My only hope was to try and break my fever with ice packs."

At that point Grandmother began to cry. "There was a small lake near where we lived. It froze over every winter. For many days, day and night, Papa went to the lake almost every hour to chop ice for ice packs. I often heard him praying as he knelt beside my bed covering me with ice packs. "God, let my daughter live. She's young. Her whole life is ahead. Take me in her place. I'm old. I've seen my day."

Grandmother paused and dried the tears from her face with her apron. Then she looked at me. Her voice was very sad as she continued. "God answered Papa's prayer. In a week I was getting well. Two weeks later Papa died of pneu-

Charles Boldreghini
Collierville, TN

monia. He was sixty seven." She took hold of my shoulders and looked into my eyes. "Remember him. He was your great grandfather. His name was Joseph."

***

Robert B. Moreland
Pleasant Prairie, WI

Hunter's Moon

Bone chilling twilight
sunset past, await moonrise;
stars withholding warmth.

Frozen ice fields crack,
bobcat prowling hungrily;
snow dampens footfalls.

Full moon apex climbs
darkest night becomes daylight;
friend, foe together.

Great horned owl questions,
mate across meadow replies;
field mice best beware!

Orion journeys
constellations attending;
stillest winter night.

Moreland, R.B. (2012) "Hunter's Moon" **Red Cedar** 2012 Vol. 14: page 43.

Judith Wenzel Andersen
Owls Head, ME

Storm Madness

When I first moved to Maine, I found my Mid-Western cheeriness severely challenged. In my past life, an innocent observation about the loveliness of the day would bring an agreement in kind. However here, a comment about beautiful weather seemed guaranteed to elicit an "Ayuh, but it is supposed to rain cats and dogs," or "Yes, but the weatherman says we are going to have a major snow." Or better yet, "Well, we are surely going to pay for it in spades." Was this that cranky Puritan history resurrected, compromising the joy of the present yet again; was it masochism; or was it just pleasure in the forced change in routine?

Weather forecasters, with their high tech tools, also seem unable to resist black warnings. Even if the week ahead is predicted to be ideal with clear skies, only enough wind to make sailors joyous, and temperatures of perfection for everyone, the dark specter of STORM ahead must be mentioned gleefully and frequently. As soon as winter officially begins, advertisements appear for weather forecasts, accompanied by music akin to the *Jaws* theme. Surely Armageddon is nigh, and woe to the meteorologist who forgets to put on the requisite sweater on snowy days.

...And then there are the random school closings which try mothers' souls. Growing up in a Chicago suburb, I never enjoyed a school shut-down for weather, except during a heat-wave of 100 plus degrees; too many students were fainting. Snowflakes did not count as a threat and school was not cancelled when our daughter went to kindergarten in the Illinois countryside, though the drifts were so high on the road that a plow bisected an abandoned car. Thus it was a shock when we moved here thirty-five years ago when our children waited pathetically in front of the house for the bus that never came, not just once, but many times; it never dawned on their mother that the State of Maine would lie

Judith Wenzel Andersen
Owls Head, ME

down and play dead when there was only the lightest dusting of white stuff floating down! Was this the Maine of hearty souls who could endure anything with flexibility and imagination? What was really strange was the mass migration of kids and their mothers to the Snow Bowl ski slopes over ghastly roads on the really nasty days. The rule seemed to be—one could risk life and limb going to ski, but not to school.

Now retired and enjoying the quiet of a snow day, it seems a nice institution, a break from the ordinary. Once here, after all of the dramatic hoopla, it is rather nice.

I still cannot help myself from mischievously telling people how gorgeous the weather is. I know what they answer will make me grin.

***

Steve Troyanovich
Florence, NJ

Ohio River Blues
for Rod Serling

the next exit
takes you to a
twilight zone oblivion
all lost tomorrows
along the way...
beyond this futile
expressway called existence
HELL is having to be
somewhere...

Laureen Haben, OSF
Milwaukee, WI

Perpetual Duel

Work of Earth and Sun spreads day to night;
when sun is farthest away:
time of unknowing, indefinable forms,
gloom coaxing evil,
eyes dilate to unreadable shapes.
Night enshrouded by Winter Solstice: fifteen hours in

        Darkness

Behold a six month's pregnancy
inched by Sun at work minute by minute.
Lit as if by taper candle's faint light,
to expel darkness,
a glowworm, light-fingered,
spreading rays, cracking dawn.
Breaking forth fire, torching,
revealing the hidden,
dispelling all feel of night
revealing, cheering, lustering.
Day is ignited:

        Light

a triumphant fifteen hours of light
for Summer Solstice has arrived.

And the sparring goes on......

Kate Leigh
Portsmouth, NH

Friendship, Maine

Overlapped seasonal cycles display
Vortices of raw elemental force.
Gale strength winds haunt the eerie winter nights,
Slender-legged currents lap summer's shores.

Remote blistered crags burst forth solid rock
Plunged with dark mica, purple garnet gems.
In tough crevices grow pale quartz and schist.
Granite inhales and exhales, as do we.

Stars above! A diamond-sprayed silken sky,
The snap of autumn, wicked fits of heat,
Demure sunsets as osprey circle fish,
Dive in devouring spirals to dinner.

Strolls by night, rests on the long wood plank dock,
Aligned with the tides, lit by the shy moon,
Autumnal equinox's balance lifts
This vespered night, spiced with our whispered lips.

**Lynne O'Leary Annis
Rockport, ME**

Picture

My mother created the color yellow with that skirt and
      jacket set,
Easter pill box hat all tweedy and spring,
Her white gloves in hand for a family picture.
Surrounding her were three little girls—my sisters and I—
Wearing different shades of blue,
Looking up at Mom, who stood all radiant and bright.
New sunglasses were spilling off our noses and white gloves
Hung in odd ways off our fingers.
We were standing on the street in front of our brown house,
Looking so proper and ready for church.
Seconds from the picture, I looked again,
And saw Mom had tamed the yellow—
But I had to spread my fingers to keep
The white gloves from sliding off.

***

**Sylvia Little-Sweat
Wingate, NC**

Grandson

Shallow newborn breaths
fill the hollow of my neck—
moth wings' soft flutter.

Genie Dailey
Jefferson, ME

Looking Up

Plumpish puffs and strands—
polyester fiberfill,
these cloud formations.

***

Night Music

That sliver of moon
sails silently over snow—
Coyote's singing.

***

Sleepless

Discomfort invades,
comes with rumbling inside me...
Oh! Baked bean supper!

Stephanie Guerin Batterman
Bath, ME

The Storm

The argument with her mother left Jane drained of energy. She had left the house after those familiar angry words. She didn't understand it really. It seemed that she and her mother could not be in the same room without tension and trouble. The sad thing was that they lived together. Jane's mother was in poor health and needed someone to look after her. No one else in the family wanted to take on the challenge of dealing with their mother's difficult temperament. Mother seemed incapable of kindness. Jane never knew why. She had never dared to question her mother. She was sure that to do so would bring too much scorn around her head and she could not face that. So, Jane lived with the constant strain of living in the same space with her mother, but every day brought the barrage of unkind words and accusations. Some days it just got too much, like today.

So she had escaped for a few moments onto the back porch. She pretended that she was checking to see if the laundry had dried. She always liked to get it in as soon as it was dry. That way the breeze would not have had a chance to blow the dust from the grassless, dirty yard onto the clothes, leaving them dirtier than before they had been washed.

Today, as she had stood there trying to calm herself, she had found a little pink flower in the dirt by the steps. She had wondered at the time how a flower could grow in that dismal place, but she had admired it and picked it, thinking that it would bring a bit of cheer to her heart. That night, when Jane went to her room, she put the flower into the cracked water glass next to her bed. She looked around the shabby room and realized that the little flower was the prettiest thing there. The light from the moon shone through the torn curtains and seemed to light the flower so that the whole room

Stephanie Guerin Batterman
Bath, ME

glowed pink. For a moment it seemed as if the room was beautiful and Jane wondered if this is what most girls saw when they went to their own rooms. But the moon shifted, the light faded, and the room returned to its shabby self. She realized then how lonely she was. She had few friends and the ones she did have she had never invited to her home, not only because of its neglected appearance, but also because of her mother. She had no idea how her mother would behave with other people, and she didn't want to take the chance of being embarrassed or having anyone find out what it was like at her house.

While she had been in school, she had stayed by herself and had to bear the whispers behind her back. She supposed the talk had been about her shyness, her poor appearance and her shabby clothes. She had never known for sure, but school had never been a happy place for her.

For years she had tried to stay clean and neat by keeping her few clothes washed and ironed in order to look like the other kids, but she knew she hadn't pulled it off. It was obvious by her patches and the few clothes that she wore that she was poor. She was so small and thin that she had been able to wear the same clothes for a couple of years in a row. That didn't help.

One day she had discovered the second-hand clothing store and that had made a big difference for her. She used the little bit of money she made baby-sitting to buy a few things. She actually discovered that she had a good eye for a kind of funky fashion. When she started wearing the things she bought there, other girls began to ask her where she shopped, but she never admitted where it was or what kind of store it was. She'd had enough humiliation.

Even some of the popular boys had begun to notice her and that had perked her up even though she had not been interested in them. Instead, what the new attention had done was make her determined to succeed. No matter what, she had decided, she would go to college and make some-

Stephanie Guerin Batterman
Bath, ME

thing of herself.

But, of course, that had all been before Bob. He had completely changed her life, even though she had only been seventeen when she met him. It was the year she would graduate from high school. He was nineteen, already out of high school, and thinking of joining up, since he wanted to fight for freedom in Vietnam. Almost everyone back then had thought that was a great idea. We had to stop Communism, and Vietnam was the place to do it. She had been so proud of him, especially after he got his uniform.

The evening that he came to pick her up in his new Army uniform was one of the proudest moments in her life. He looked so handsome that when he told her that he would love her forever, her heart simply melted. She couldn't help it. She gave herself to him in a rush of passion that surprised them both. Afterward, he held her and told her not to be afraid. She could go to college while he was away and when he returned, they would live a wonderful life together

Bob never returned from that war. That was how her happiest hopes had led her to her present despair. She had been left alone—alone with her mother. College had never happened. After Bob's death, she had given up—given up her dream—given up hope. It didn't seem fair. After that latest fight with her mother, Jane was filled with a new mourning and a strange longing. She turned over in her bed, in her shabby room and hid her face in her pillow to muffle her sobs. She fell asleep with tears staining her pillow.

She awoke in the middle of the night to the cold stinging odor of an impending storm. Quickly she moved from the bed to the window to close it against the cold. It was too late, of course. The room was already icy cold. She shivered in her thin flannel nightgown and tried to take a deep breath, but the frosty air cut her breath short. She moved to the other side of the window to be nearer the heat register.

The window in her third floor bedroom gave her a bird's eye view of the landscape before her. She could see a row of

Stephanie Guerin Batterman
Bath, ME

black, naked trees close to the house. Their trunks formed vertical lines which contrasted with the zig-zagging irregularity of the trees' branches and twigs. Behind the line of trees, across the river, lay an ocean of fuzzy, almost fur-like, gray treetops. The horizon was formed by the meeting of the gray fur with the blackness of the restless clouds above.

As she watched, all was motionless in seeming anticipation of impending danger. All was blackness and foreboding. It was as if the whole world were waiting, waiting for the storm to break. Even her heart was beating in time to this mysterious waiting.

She wanted to run, to return to her warm bed and forget what was happening outside, but her feet seemed frozen to the spot. She knew that she should go check on her mother to be sure that she was sleeping, but she could not bear the thought of another argument. She could only stand there, watching and dreading the storm to come. She had weathered storms before and had certainly survived them. She did not understand what force held her there in awful anticipation. Maybe it was the memory of her argument with her mother. Maybe the coming storm was a bit like walking into a room that her mother occupied.

Suddenly, the clouds opened, pouring forth their burden in the form of large, white, whirling flakes. The first of them struck the window with unexpected force and she trembled in fear. The flakes melted as they struck the warmth of the window and streamed down the pain forming rivulets of moisture which quickly froze into complex patterns of frost and ice.

The distant view was lost in the blanket of whiteness that enfolded it. The black lines of the nearby tree trunks became grotesquely distorted by the window's frost and ice. They seemed to gyrate before her eyes in some kind of evil primitive dance.

She stood at the window entranced, her pulse beating to the rhythm of the world outside. Somehow the violence of the

Stephanie Guerin Batterman
Bath, ME

storm matched her inner world, the secret world where she lived her real life. This was the world of pain and regret. This was the world of lost love and lost hope. This was the inner landscape that was her reality.

She did not know how long the storm lasted. It stopped as suddenly as it had begun. The sky slowly lost its blackness as the clouds receded. The moon shone and revealed the treetops which had been left with a blanket of pure white snow that sparked and danced in the light. She breathed deeply and noticed how the world had been transformed into one of perfect whiteness and purity. She imagined that the same transformation had taken place in her heart.

Yes, the world had been unkind. Yes, her mother had been unkind. Yes, she had despaired of her dreams. It seemed as if a storm had been raging in her heart and mind for many years, but seeing the world transformed somehow gave her a glimmer of hope. She breathed again allowing herself to begin to embrace this change.

It was then that she realized how very tired and cold she was. She returned to her bed, covered herself with her tattered quilt. For the first time in years she slept without wondering what troubles tomorrow would bring or what complaints she would have to endure from her mother.

Maybe tomorrow will be better, she thought. *Maybe tomorrow the storm will have passed and I can begin again.*

For once in a very long time, she simply slept.

Earl Weigelt
Winslow, ME

Alacarte

Why so tepid, squeamish,
so enamored of a nebulous Transcendent?
Such coziness have we with the indeterminate
that we'd rather Divinity remain that way?

Prefer the Watchmaker to lock his doors and pull
the drapes than walk his cart down the street?
Gauche is it, for Him to hawk His wares?

No one would accuse the Almighty of being
Rude!
Certainly not brash
nor intolerant nor scrutinizing!

Far be it from Him to expect anything of us!

Surely the Other would not stoop
nor diminish Himself
to this lowly plain,
to dirt and sweat
and blood and wood!

Kate Leigh
Portsmouth, NH

Southern Slice

From a crevice worn and wide,
Where the smooth sand slopes aside,

See I clear an island fair,
There a white spire marks the air.

There the weighty rock has split;
The lone access but a spit.

Where the lighthouse keeper lived,
Beams of warning ships to give.

The lap of waves that sing to me,
The deep blue ripples on the sea,

The wet slick weed, the smell of salt,
The clouds slow drift without halt,

The shadow of the gull above,
Combine to offer all I love.

The pungent sound of distant bell,
The soothing call I know so well.

The patterned wing, the fine-etched rock,
The severe beak, each granite block

Speaks aloud to tiny me,
Drawn in ever by the sea.

Here between these sunken walls,
A timeless sense holds me in thrall;

I might exist, or maybe not,
As long and lone I feel this spot.

Jean Lawrence
Waldoboro, ME

Maude Clark Gay
1876-1962

The ninety plus lady closed her eyes and said,
"Click, click; Tap, tap! I can still hear Maude's heels
As she hurried down the hill to pick up her paper at the
      store where I worked."
And the eighty-eight year old lady said,
"Oh, Maude's hats and stylish dress! She was the classiest
      woman in town!"
And the third, interviewed,
"Tea at Maude's was something special.
I was only a little girl, but I knew it was an event to be
      savored."

Few in our village today remember Maude Clark Gay, for
      she left us years ago.
The first to stand in line in 1919 when women were finally
      allowed to vote,
Secretary of the WWI Home Effort to support the troops,
Writer of several works of fiction, collector and teller of
      coastal tales,
Wife to one of the town's most successful businessmen,
      devoted mother,
First woman from Waldoboro to serve in the Maine House
      ('29) and Senate ('33),
Maude shone brightly in our small town and accomplished
      much in her lifetime.
For many, this might have been enough!

But her story doesn't end there.
Joining the Waldoboro Woman's Club at the early age of
      sixteen, where her abilities were recognized.

(continued)

Goose River Anthology, 2013// 130

Jean Lawrence
Waldoboro, ME

She rose from local president to President of the Lincoln
    County Woman's Clubs.
Moving on to the Maine Federation of Woman's Clubs, she
    became State President ('37-'39),
Traveled the State extensively, and through her articles,
Informed the public of bills pending in the Legislature.
While travelling throughout the country displaying her
    lovely hats, charming personality and leadership,
She continued to promote the ideals of her organization.

A credit to her family, hometown, and State,
Maude was a model of good citizenship within an active
    lifestyle.
Her life was a template for the many women who knew her
    and followed in her footsteps.

***

Peggy Gannon
Palmyra, ME

End of a Season

Who can tell
crusted with the glaze of winter
what the rose may know?
We have forgotten
all that the earth taught us when we were children.
Petals that once wrapped us
now have fallen from us.
Naked we go
into the blinding snow.

Goose River Anthology, 2013//131

Thomas C. Collins
New Harbor, ME

Wonderful Winston

Winston, the wonder dog,
walks on all his legs,
but dances with only two.

Lots of sleep is normal,
and running normal too,
for wonderful Winston.

Powder puff white
with curly tale,
Winston's a pure delight.

He loves to chew,
licks a lot, and
dreams through the night.

Best of all, he loves me.
And I love him too, you see.

***

Where They Go

All my tangible personal property
goes to my wife, if she survives me,
or my trust if she doesn't.
But my loves, fears, hopes,
imaginings and future plans?
Those I'm taking with me.

Goose River Anthology, 2013//132

Dorothy Weiss
Orlando, FL

Gifts

My sister-in law, Lillian, shares her experiences and photographs with me frequently through email. I asked her to consider writing a story about this experience, but she answered, "You write it, you have my permission. You love to write. It's a gift. You write the story."

Lillian works in an office in a brownstone near a university campus. In the back of the brownstone house there is a deck. One morning she saw a mother cat outside on the deck with three kittens: a solid black one, a gold one and a striped black and gold one. The mother cat looked so scrawny trying to nurse her kittens that Lillian felt sorry for her. She brought some milk, some dry food and some wet food, and started feeding the cat. Finding these beautiful little creatures on her first day back at work was a pleasant surprise and somehow uplifting. Her mother had just died. She was still grieving. *Where had they come from? How did they get there?*

As the weeks went by, Lillian found herself completely captivated by these cats. The mother cat kept her kittens tucked protectively under the deck at night. During the day, she carried them over onto the deck one by one in her mouth to feed them, and it seemed to also keep a watchful eye on Lillian and her colleagues at work. They would look out at the kittens, smile, join them briefly on their lunch break and then go back to work. When they closed the office to leave at the end of the day, they could see the mother cat taking her kittens back under the deck and out of sight.

One day it was pouring rain, the kittens had grown bigger and were too heavy for the mother cat to carry them up and over onto the deck. Lillian thought if only she had a plank the kittens could walk on it and climb up and onto the deck themselves. But she didn't have a plank. At lunch time,

Dorothy Weiss
Orlando, FL

it was still raining. Two of the ladies decided to go out to eat at a local restaurant and left Lillian still wondering what to do about the kittens in the rain. Minutes later the ladies returned with a plank that they just happened to find laying in the street. It was actually a board with a filter on it, but it was strong enough for the kittens to walk up and over onto the deck and out of the rain.

The mother cat leaped over onto the deck and joined her kittens. She looked at Lillian and her colleagues and purred her approval of their actions. They were amazed that this board appeared in the street so promptly right after it was needed. "Ask and it shall be given," one of the ladies murmured. They couldn't help but believe they had received a sign from heaven to continue taking care of these little creatures.

The very next day from her office window, Lillian watched the kittens. They were curious and frisky, flexing their independence. One of them jumped from the deck of the other brownstone house on the left up and onto her office deck. It happened so fast, the kitten resembled a ball of fur flying through the air. It landed safely on all four paws, shook itself and meowed with delight. The other two kittens did the same thing, bouncing into the air and landing easily onto the deck—so Lillian threw the plank away as the kittens had discovered another facet of their strength, and no longer needed it. They were like living springboards themselves—flipping, jumping, climbing, and spinning around. Clearly, they no longer needed the plank or the mother cat. They were already eating on their own from the food the ladies put out on the deck.

After a while, the mother cat appeared occasionally, but not as often. She watched her kittens antics from a distance as they grew larger and larger and demonstrated their skills: cleaning themselves, finding their own food, and exploring other areas further away from the deck and the brownstone buildings. Then one day the mother cat quietly slipped away

Dorothy Weiss
Orlando, FL

and never returned. Someone took one of the kittens but Lillian and her colleagues still have Blondie and Goldie.

I continue to speculate about the wonder of nature going on as usual in the animal kingdom in the heart of a busy urban city, teeming with humans, traffic, and noise. I tend to think of cats on farms roaming through the meadow chasing birds and rabbits, peering through windows, mischievously. But here in the city, these cats were doing pretty much the same, without fear. Remarkable. Like a human mom, the mother cat nurtured, protected, and taught her babies about survival, watched them grow and become capable of taking care of themselves. When necessary, she found and accepted help from humans. She placed her babies where Lillian and her colleagues could see them and assist her in caring for them. Then as if by some mystical predestined date and time, when her babies were mature enough, the mother cat let go of them. She slipped away, allowing them to go on living without her; her purpose completed. Much like human beings and the universal circle of life. Helping the cats seemed to help Lillian re-energize, re-focus, and get back into living life fully, easing her sorrow as the days went by.

I think about my own mother, her unconditional love and many sacrifices. She is long gone, but not forgotten. Yes, gifts come in all assorted sizes and shapes and forms. Some gifts are in human form, others are beautifully crafted and presented by nature.

Peggy Trojan
Brule, WI

November 5, 1915

Cooling herself after baking bread
on the wood stove late at night,
my grandmother was
found dead on the stoop.
Mother was nine.

Days before,
walking together on the short cut.
Grandmother stopped
to make a cairn of rocks.
"A memorial," she said.

Children on the homestead
were expected to be strong,
to understand death
is a necessary part of living.

I asked Mother once
if she had been very sad,
lost and lonely.
She said "No,"
she was cared for,
being the last of eight.
Life on the farm went on.

All her long life,
she felt for little beings:
helpless people, hurt animals.

And she collected rocks,
which, easily found,
last forever.

Sharon Auberle
Sister Bay, WI

November, Snow & Roses
for Lucha

I came bearing tea, bread and poetry to talk about sadness
this rain-slashed afternoon.
*It's the leaves, you said, they let go so gently this late in the
year as if, finally, they have accepted...*

We watched, saying nothing for a while. You showed me
tamarack blazing against gray skies, the brilliant yellow of
asparagus ferns in wet grasses. I know you will paint these
one day, as you knew I would write these words.

A fat squirrel lumbered up and down the feeder, storing up
for winter. He made us laugh but sadness, sweet melan-
choly returned. Sometimes it's all too beautiful to bear...

Tonight there are first whirling snowflakes. Among them
still shimmers a scarlet shrub, though last week there was
a hard frost. In the bush two roses are blooming fresh and
bright, even a third buds in the snow.

We do not expect these gifts in November. So much we
don't expect in this life...
how bravely flowers can bloom in winter...how sorrow can
reside so near to joy...how sometimes they can be the
same.

> *snow and roses*
> *an old man in a red cap*
> *stops and smiles*

George Wentz
Sturgeon Bay, WI

Morning After a Spring Snow

Ribbons of snow blown by the wind
formed sculpted drifts beside the road,
wrinkles in a fresh white blanket
that covered the countryside.

The peaceful scene of nature's art
painted along the rural churchyard fence,
where souls had found their eternal rest
guarded by marble angels and giant oaks.

On this early morn, beneath one headstone,
a visitor had already been
leaving an inscription in the fresh snow
that simply said—"Love."

A tender message from a lonely heart
left to seep slowly into the earth
under the sun's warm rays, reaching down
with thoughts and memories from above.

Nancy Freund Bills
South Portland, ME

The Family Table

Even in early winter, a high drift of Maine snow almost covers the north-facing windows of my family's dining room. In the dim inches of natural light, I watch my husband, Geoff, tilt the "family table" on its side, then upend it entirely. The mahogany bentwood legs of the table are laid bare and appear vulnerable in the chilly room.

My mother-in-law has entrusted the family table to us. For me, it's a treasure and for Geoff, a hand-me-down. She's given me her instructions, "The tabletop needs refinishing. Surely, there's someone in your area who can do it." And I've contacted "a good man in Fort Fairfield."

Geoff and I kneel on the dining room's wide pine floorboards beside the table. For a moment, the plaid back of his flannel shirt blocks my view of his face; I remember rather than see his beard and mustache. His hazel eyes study the table's underpinnings. Then, he rises abruptly and sets the table upright. I stand and watch him while by touch alone, he slips a flat-head screwdriver under the tabletop and searches for and finds the threadbare holes. Rust and wood fibers begin to fall like food crumbs on the bare floorboards. I gather each screw as it falls. As the family table, the witness of innumerable birthdays and anniversaries, is pried apart, I hear the splintering of wood; the veteran of family Sunday dinners groans.

I hear a brief intake of air, a sucking sound. It's me.

With his arms spread wide as a hawk's, Geoff lifts the large round tabletop off its base and rests it against a door frame. The scarce light is disappearing; I flick on the overhead light—harsh, yellow, rarely used, to reassure myself that the dining room is still there. The stenciled flowers—red, green and yellow, along the chair rail, a labor of love of hundreds of hours, remain. In the empty room where the antique

Nancy Freund Bills
South Portland, ME

table has been disassembled, sundered, the blooms are like an eerie halo amid mortal blows.

I turn off the light as I hear Geoff roll the tabletop across the linoleum of the hallway, the kitchen, the entry. I imagine the child-scarred edges pass through grit, dog hair, even the remnants of red sauce. It will be virtually unscathed, but I hear Geoff hesitate when faced with the snow on the porch, the ice and gravel on the driveway.

Geoff's voice rises, and it travels through the maze of the old farmhouse hallways. "It won't fit," he calls to me. "It" being the tabletop. And I understand; the original plan must be altered.

"It won't fit inside," he calls out again. "I'll have to tie it on top."

I make it to the snowy porch off the kitchen and wince watching the tabletop lifted carelessly onto the Volkswagen Campmobile's roof, tied with haphazard loops and knots of clothesline. Then I duck my head under a low-hanging door-jamb, hide in the pantry, and whisper to the shelves of canned soup and fruit, "I've sewn tablecloths, polished the silver, roasted the turkeys....And I hoped the family table could be refinished. But now, it's up to Geoff."

I hear Geoff swear and the exaggerated slam of car doors. By the time I reach the kitchen windows, the Campmobile with its awkward and bizarre load is disappearing down our steep driveway and into the late afternoon grey.

On the road from Caribou to Fort Fairfield, the round tabletop levitates like a flying saucer above the box-like vehicle. Around curves, beside defoliated potato fields, it tests the air currents to the south and then to the north. Between test flights, it makes soft irregular thumps on the car roof while the Campmobile's top bunk, no more than a hammock, sways.

Then, the rural route dips and swings sharply in a crow's flight toward New Brunswick. Right after the Magnusons' barn, the tabletop like a discus, lifts off the Volkswagen's

Nancy Freund Bills
South Portland, ME

roof, it vibrates momentarily in space. It shudders, flutters, trembles. But it flies.

For a few hopeful moments, the bloody brown sinews of mahogany are blessedly saved from consequence. But after that limbo, the tabletop dives toward hard-rutted ground, strikes the potato field with sickening force, and scatters its integrity among the powdered leaves and rotten tubers.

Geoff is surprised. He responds like a farmer startled by a natural disaster; like a husbandman he realizes that his crop is ruined. While pacing up and down uneven rows of blackened potato leaves, he finds cracked limbs and shattered fragments of wing. His hands raise, examine, and then drop the table's bones and body parts—tibias, a scapula, and a pharynx.

And I scream. When I hear. No, I am silent. After all, I witnessed the dissolving of the seal between the foundation and the monument. The family table is shattered. And I know it will never again be intact.

***

Patrick T. Randolph
Kalamazoo, MI

Reflections

Businessman's

    Shiny shoes—

        Poor man's mirror.

Peggy Gannon
Palmyra, ME

Mrs. Grundy's Garden

                              ...just won't quit.
The Missus has been gone these thirteen years
and Gordon Grundy didn't seem to cotton
to the effulgence in his own front yard.
So it went wild. The shoots shot upright,
the trailers spread and sprawled, the ramblers rambled,
everything thriving with wild abandon.
From the moist rich earthworm-tumbled leaf mold
of spring, spring the bulbs: tulips, crocuses,
daffodils, sprouting defiance of winter.
Mrs. Grundy planted them after the War,
a kind of celebration of life, a kind of
resurrection, a kept promise, sure as the
flooding of the Nile. Yes, they're unstoppable.

She was still young when she set the roses out
because a woman with one at the breast, one
at her side, and one in the pipeline
has a special need
for the fragrance they surrender to the evening.

And wasn't it Mr. Grundy who gave her
the purple lilac bush one Mother's Day?
He saw it all, but never let it move him.
Sprays of bleeding heart by the back door
linger into June.
Forget-me-nots have scattered their seed randomly,
delicate drifts of blue. Later come the daylilies:
over the years they've abandoned their front lines
down the ditch and clear across the road—
assertive, steadfast soldiers, marching forward.

(continued)

Peggy Gannon
Palmyra, ME

Tiger lilies tower above them, aloof.
In August there's a smoketree that explodes
in plumes and puffs of purple by the roadside,
far too exotic for a Maine garden.

Every gardener knows, the sole intent
of a garden is to turn itself into a meadow
the minute your back is turned. In recent years,
Mrs. Grundy's arthritic hands unable
to combat the encroaching weeds and grasses,
the inevitable reversion began,
a slow decline.
When she surrendered to the dark hereafter,
she seemed to have imparted something
of her staunch, persistent spirit to her garden.
Her flowers just refused to disappear.

Old Mr. Grundy, ridden with the palsy,
followed her at last, and then the house
was taken over by the dogcatcher
who didn't know a pansy from a potato.
One day a trailer appeared in the back yard
and the dogcatcher's things were moved to the trailer
and the antique dealer took his pick of the leavings
and then the tired old center-chimney cape
was knocked to the ground and burned.

                       Out of the ashes
forget-me-nots and creeping phlox run wild,
Virginia Creeper sprawls, the brambles ramble.
Mrs. Grundy's garden just won't quit.

Stephanie Noyes McSherry
Edgecomb, ME

Cathedral Woods

Sunlight penetrates the forest
of evergreen and ash.
A brilliant golden glow
Envelops visitors
to this sacred space,
where fairies frolic in whispers.

Three generations explore the woods
with respect and wonder,
marveling at the beauty of nature,
and what gifts
others have left behind.

It is a familiar place,
and they settle down,
amidst the moss and dry oranged pine needles,
to unpack the treasures they have gathered
along the beach, and on the journey
into the woods.

Seaglass—blue, green, white, brown
Cut yellow flowers, pruned that morning,
from the garden of the café by the ferry dock.
Ferns and fallen leaves and empty lobster shells,
Small stones and sticks,
Mussel, clam and scallop shells

All conspire to create
the splendid fairy house,
Touched with the warmth and love
of the three generations
grateful for this day—and one another—
in the shelter of Cathedral Woods.

Jeanne Severin-Hansen
Knightdale, NC

Dinner at Our House

Dinner at our house was sacred family time. Around the table we sat. Left over bits of liver or some other ungodly concoction shimmered, waiting to be thrown out or given to the dog. "Eat your dinner, people are starving in Calcutta," was a constant refrain heard at dinner time. I left the codfish-liver-chipped beef on toast-whatever and ate thirds of vegetables. I'm full. More goop was pushed onto my plate until I cry and go to bed without being told. Alone was better than facing a determined matriarch. The scene played itself out on a nightly basis. Years later, I still hear the litany, see the scene, and smell the leftovers we were forced to eat. One night I boxed up dinner and addressed it: Starving Person, Calcutta, India.

After that dinner looked more normal. The undertone of eat what's on your plate never went away. Neither did the incessant guilt trip of two hard-working parents providing for an ungrateful child. Now there was a polite veneer and normal food. Hamburger and spaghetti followed by vanilla pudding. But only if you ate your plate down to the last morsel. If I'd have eaten the portions delivered nightly I never would have had enough room for dessert. The dog became my best friend and the plate was always clean. I couldn't beat my mother and I wasn't going to play her game. So I played my own game and used her rules.

I still won't eat at a Formica table in a small kitchen crowded with pots and pans. There she was, the Donna Reed look-alike. Always smiling and pretty, asking endless, nosey questions. Prying down, ever down into the me I prefer to keep to myself. Dinner at my house was always sacred family time. Norman Rockwell sits the four of us down and don't we look pretty. Two girls with scrubbed faces and clean hands and Mom dishing out more mashed potatoes. Dad

Jeanne Severin-Hansen
Knightdale, NC

occupied his corner, smirking and chomping ever harder on his pipe or fiddling with the change in his pocket.

Don't we look nice? Just don't look too closely. Don't stop to see what's really going on. Every night at six the pantomime began and every night at seven there were unspoken winners and losers in an ongoing battle waged over food so politely and prettily served. The older I got the better I played, enlisting siblings and eventually patriarchal participation. Dinner at our house ended finally when I left home. Now I eat what, when, and where I want.

***

Sylvia Little-Sweat
Wingate, NC

Old Salts

Like old fishermen
who gather to swap
seafaring stories,
pelicans stand
on sandbars to face
the morning sun.
They squat and squawk
their claims to turf.
When warm they soar
over the surf's roar
to dive for fish
like kamikazes.

Mary Jo Balistreri
Waukesha, WI

For My Father at Ninety-Three
after Frantisek Kupka, Shades of Violet

With the thousand-year-old voice of oceans,
his words curl like smoke in the powder
blue stillness.
It is late afternoon, his favorite time
of day, when the sky goes soft
and sun cloaks his body in violet alpenglow.

He basks in the warmth of age,
does not pine for the coiled energy of youth,
the white-hot heat and fiery flame.
Tension and stress
compressed and layered
now part of his history.

He rises in quiet, anchored by earth, blessed by sky.
His adamant body lets go of all
but the essential.
He accepts his stone self,
makes peace with water's wear, wind's abrasion.
He carries his shaping nowhere,
everywhere,
a phoenix in the scarlet flames of the sun.

Christina McIntyre
Augusta, ME

Those Awful Little Words

The way that I feel is so sad and so real.
My heart aches from the pain
My thoughts scream out your name

Just hours ago
I heard your voice on the phone
And I can still remember the last words that you told.

It was silly of us to argue
I was wrong and I'm so sorry
I told you that I hated you

And said we shouldn't be
And even after all of this
You still said that you loved me

Angry and frustrated
I quickly stopped the call
I swore I'd never see you

I refused to take your calls
That evening after I calmed down
I listened to your message

You said you'd always love me
You said you'd never leave
You told me I was special

And you told me you forgave me
I realized that I missed you
I called you right away

Christina McIntyre
Augusta, ME

I wanted us to be together
And to never part
I smiled as you answered

But the voice it wasn't yours
A stranger never heard before
A sense of fear came from his words

He told me he was sorry
He wished the worse was over
He told me of the Accident

That took your life forever
And as I listened to his words
My eyes began to swell

And all that I could remember
Was the last thing that was spoken
When I told you that I hated you

And I swore I'd never see you
If I knew that this would be
The last thing we would share

I would have told you how I really felt
I would have told you I was wrong
I would have told you that I loved you

And that you were right all along
But now I'll always remember
Those awful little words

The ones that I said to you
The night you left this world.

T.A. Cullen
Madison, WI

Space Jump

Some guy dropped 24 miles out of the sky
and according to all reports landed on his feet.
Two hours up, 10 minutes down and don't die.
No room for panic or truth, just a real sweet

thrill. The pursuit of destiny without any control.
Cowboys skipping from broncos and bulls,
passing into space fall dreams, beyond the toll
of church bells that scream into a dull

black hole in space where our voices
are swallowed as we whisper about chance
and the probability and the crazy choice
to grab the red- headed girl and dance

till we all drop any insane aspiration
and leave behind all that quiet desperation.

***

Patrick T. Randolph
Kalamazoo, MI

Up North

Our shadows—

         Drunk with night—

                  Hug every tree.

Alexa Patterson
Lanark, IL

Healed With Time

My name is Serena Cartwright and this is my story.

Five years ago something changed me, for the better and for the worse. Everything seemed fine—normal even—and then in one second everything changed. Like when the flash on a camera goes off and you're momentarily blinded. But once your vision clears, you see that something isn't right. *Something changed.* I didn't understand it; I still don't. But I just know people do things for reasons unforeseeable to most of us, but in time even the most dangerous secrets do come out.

It all started five years ago when I was riding in the car with my parents. We were driving across the Golden Gate Bridge. I felt like something was off…something about the picture I was looking at wasn't making sense. Then I finally noticed what was strange, Black SUVs with dark tinted windows blocked the road on either end of the bridge. Men dressed all in black started piling out of the cars…and they had *guns.* Like fish in a barrel, we were trapped. I took out my cell phone and dialed 911, still so unbelievably calm for a situation like this.

Someone answered and I hurriedly described my situation. She asked for my location and I told her we were on the Golden Gate Bridge. She paused before telling me, in the most irritating manner I have ever heard, to prank call someone else.

Then she hung up.

That was my last lifeline; I didn't know that at the time, but something tells me I should have suspected it.

The men in black—the ones with the very deadly looking guns—ordered all of us to get out of our cars. They lined us all up on the side of the bridge. They scrutinized every one of

Alexa Patterson
Lanark, IL

us before passing onto the next person. When the man—who I assumed was the leader—came to us I noticed the wicked grin donned upon his face. He seemed to enjoy everyone's terror; too much to be sane. He yelled something to his men in a language I didn't recognize and they all strode back to their SUVs. They didn't leave though. They were discussing something; that I could tell by the obvious glances toward all of us lined up side-by-side. I knew something was wrong, but what could I do about it?

I looked from my left to my right, slowly; calculating. I tried to find a solution to this soon to be fatal problem. But nothing jumped out at me. The clock was ticking and I was running out of time...that was all I knew. Before I could think anything else, an ear shattering boom sounded and the bridge shuddered. I blacked out then, and that's all I remember.

I woke up lying on a stretcher at the end of the bridge. I remember opening my eyes to a dull, gray sky and looking to my left I saw what would soon haunt me forever. Where the bridge used to be was now a gaping hole, dropping off sharply into the turbulent waters below. The massive towers of steel that formerly suspended the bridge were now blackened and still smoking. They protruded from the water like giant teeth, as if it was the sea's horrendous mouth. It was the perfect picture of destruction.

I won't linger too much on this part of the story, for it still pains me so much to remember it.

I don't recall feeling anything...I was simply empty; numb and unfeeling. How could I care about anything when all I had ever cared for was gone from now on, never to be seen again? They tried talking to me, asking me questions; to which I didn't respond. I was taken to the hospital; where I was prodded, poked, and questioned until they were tired of my lack of response.

I remember that night very clearly. Unable to sleep, I laid still and listened. I heard echoing footsteps in the hall and

Alexa Patterson
Lanark, IL

their abrupt end outside my door. An argument about me, something I did not know at the time, pierced through the twilight's darkness. A man—who I later found out was the resident therapist—and a woman's harsh whispers were heard in the hall.

That day...that day my life changed, whether I accepted it or not. From then on nothing was ever the same.

That next day I met the woman who was speaking out in the hall the night before. When she walked in I was momentarily shocked by the resemblance between us. She, unbelievably enough, looked just like an older version of me. The only difference that I could find was our eyes. Hers a warm brown while mine are a steely gray.

Her name was Bethan.

She claimed to be my mother's sister.

I wouldn't listen to her.

My mother told me she never had a sister. Oh, but she was my mother's sister...that and so much more... I had believed my mother never lied, oh how wrong I was...

I spent four days in that hospital.

The longest and most dreadful four days I have yet to endure.

Against my will, I was sent to live with my supposed "aunt." I hated it at first; but then again...at that time I hated the world. For the world took the only two people I had ever loved and cared for away from me. After some time I grew content with being there, I even—dare I say it?—enjoyed it at times.

Many secrets formerly kept in the dark were brought into the light while I stayed with my aunt.

The biggest secret being about my Aunt Bethan. She had cancer... and only *five months to live* starting from the time she took me in. After learning of that I treasured our time together. She proved to be so caring and kind. Always soft spoken and never raised her voice. I started looking forward to our special times together, sitting by the warm fireplace

Alexa Patterson
Lanark, IL

and trading stories. I cherished those moments the most.

Then her condition worsened and she was confined to the hospital. They said it was a matter of days before she died. I couldn't bear the thought of another one I love's time ticking away on the clock of life. I began to hate time, the very essence of it. It was a reminder of the seconds that were ticking down on her life; each second could be her last. So in a fit of frustration at the world I broke every clock in the house. I couldn't stand seeing the seconds tick by, counting down on her life.

I wished time would freeze, but my wish was not granted. All too soon, cruel fate took her, too, from this world. I was crushed by her death, more so since I knew it was coming and couldn't become numb from the shock of it like with my parents. And this time I had no support, no will to go on while everyone I ever cared for were never to be found again.

But one day all that changed. I found out another life-changing secret that helped me find the will to go on and search for something...someone.

It happened when I was cleaning out the attic in my late aunt's house. I was carrying a box down the stairs when I tripped and fell. The box tumbled down the stairs, spilling out its contents along the way. As I mindlessly picked up the various papers littering the steps I came across one in particular, that gave me all the hope in the world and crushed me all at once.

It was a birth certificate...*my birth certificate*. I was not Priscilla's, my mother's, child.... I was *Bethan's*. And who I thought was my father, James, was not my actual father. Instead my father was a...William Fitzgerald.

My whole world stopped right there, everything I thought I knew turned out to be a lie. Missing pieces soon clicked into the puzzle that was my life. That changed things for me; I could still have someone related by blood to me here. Here and...*alive.*

I resolved to search for William Fitzgerald and I soon

Alexa Patterson
Lanark, IL

found out everything I could about him, *my real father*. And before I could second guess myself I was on a plane to London to find him. I didn't have to search long to find him, for he was quite known in London. But it took me a while to gain the courage to go see him. And when I finally did I found out....he didn't know who I was.

He was a politician, and a very important one. I couldn't tell him, by doing so I would ruin his carrier. If news went around that I was his daughter, it would become a scandal. Every headline would boast the inside story about the latest and greatest scandal. Rumors would fly and William's life would be upended into complete disorder. And everything he had worked for would be all for not. So I couldn't tell him.

But knowing I still had some family out there—alive—I eventually succumbed to the desire to know my real father and told him. It was kept a secret, though, not even his closest advisors knew of my existence. He told me about his relationship with Bethan; he had known her a long time ago, he dated her for a while, before his politics got in the way of their relationship and they broke it off. He was wary around me; I began to believe that he didn't want me. I was right.

In fear that the secret might get out—and the hope that there was a chance that he wasn't my real father—led him to take a blood test and...it didn't match up. *I wasn't William Fitzgerald's daughter.*

To say I was disappointed was an understatement. I still didn't know my *real father*. But I had to keep searching, I couldn't stop now. I couldn't stop until I found my real father.

I researched everyone Bethan had been in contact with around the time I was born. And soon, I found something concrete; *she had a husband*. It was a possibility that I was the daughter of an eccentric photographer named Kevin Night who lived in Hawaii. I searched for him for a year; half of that time was again spent gaining the courage to go meet him. When I first met him, I could see the profound resem-

Alexa Patterson
Lanark, IL

blance between us; we shared the same steely gray eyes that I never found on any of my relatives.

He told me he married Bethan a year before I was born.

He never knew about me.

He kept up a long distance relationship with Bethan, through the unconventional use of letters. The reason for the long distance relationship being that he moved to Hawaii, but Bethan chose not to go with him. He still loved her dearly though. He had often wondered why her letters abruptly stopped three years ago. I had to break the news to him that she had died; he never even knew she had cancer. The news devastated him terribly...

I was hesitant at first, not wanting to care for someone only to have them ripped out of my life once again. But eventually I did come to care for him, I accepted him as my father and he happily accepted me as his daughter.

Two years later and here I am, living in a small house on a secluded part of the beach with my *real* father. I often think back on my past, all that I have learned and lived through. There were some very hard times in my past. But I made it through them, didn't I? And I lived to tell the tale. Others didn't, but they continue to live on in my thoughts and my heart always. Even though some piece of paper states my parents were not who I thought they were, when I think of my parents I will always remember Priscilla and James Cartwright. I have learned some very hard lessons...The truth always hurts...but it sets you free. Time is something that should be treasured and *never* taken for granted. Two things all of us should remember from this are that time has the value of gold...and secrets should never be shadows.

Laureen Haben, OSF
Milwaukee, WI

Cherry Blossoms

An emblem of love and good fortune
flowering cherry trees also
continue as an enduring metaphor
for "the fleeting nature of life."

Imperial Japan of long ago
planted cherry trees
when claiming
occupied territory.

Now blossoms adorn
coins, kimonos and stationery
to nurture
Japanese spirit.

In a long ago time, cherry trees were gifted
(and later replenished)
to the United States to celebrate
the nations' then-growing friendship.

Approaching the vernal equinox
we eagerly look to Washington
for the pink-tinged white blossoms
announcing the arrival of spring.

And for some the time-honored practice
endures as they picnic
under the glorious array
of the *sakura* trees.

Cindy Partington
Des Moines, IA

March Moments

the moment you took off
for "parts unknown"
tornadic storms rolled through
then day after day
thick clouds turned day into twilight
damp haze buffered every noise
we peered through the gauze
softening the river, the woods,
the regimented rows of crosses
while the military organized
their recording of taps,
assigned flag presentation duty
while we arranged
our temporary good-bye
unrelenting cold mist
dampened our faces
as we gathered, cried,
slipped into our cars

unable to leave town
without one last moment of connection
we two returned
another darkened day
shoes in freshly turned moist dirt
we sent our silent messages
into the unknown

felt before seen
warming momentary sunbeams
broke through
a porthole in the swirling gray

(continued)

Cindy Partington
Des Moines, IA

like a sudden spotlight
enclosing us in its circle
turning water drops
to glistening multicolored orbs
we turned our faces heavenward
and stretched our arms wide
absorbing
then shook our heads in wonder
when the gift dissipated

***

Genie Dailey
Jefferson, ME

In Fog

I wake to unexpected fog.
Daybreak trees, gray-green silhouettes,
Implore a creamy, lightening sky.
Silent birdsong; standstill breeze; the mist unmoving—
I must go out!

Swinging arms/swirling air,
I walk/fog stalks,
Curling away then folding behind me.
I turn to catch its embrace—
An illusion!

Sherry Ballou Hanson
Brunswick, ME

Eternal Rhythm

Back in time when I did not know so much
or so little, when stars stood taller
or my eyes were better, when those stars
represented where I might go one day,
when the salty sea brought health
and the wind carried my dreams...life
seemed everlasting when I was young
when I did not know it wasn't me that was wrong
but them, so much I did not know and just as well.

Earth has laid down to rest this spare December morning
and a pale sun slants off frosted tufts of grass
alongside the old stone fort by the sea. Some of us
come to resemble the Maine winter: spare and
wind-scoured, focused toward survival when trees are bare
and blue jays, chickadees and a cardinal haunt our feeders.

Winter is at low flame and we huddle in fragile light
on the exposed ledges of January and February,
          while March
floats a low band of smoke gray cloud at horizon.
Eighteen degrees and shadows stretch long. Six ducks
undulate on a cobalt sea and gulls circle watching for fish.
They have better eyes then mine these days
and maybe that is a good thing.

J. Adams
Edgecomb, ME

Things Remembered

Winter was a great time when growing up on a farm. This was the time of year when we took to the woods to harvest next winter's heat. It was a wondrous time filled with joy and excitement that came through hard work. We used oxen as our mode of transportation to haul the wood and supplies. Oxen are well suited for this type of work and are a source of comfort during a day in the woods.

Our woodlot was a trek from the warm safety of the barn through glistening fields of white. A simple trail groomed by a chain dragged behind the sled created a nice road for winter's work. We drove our oxen with reins during those months, allowing for a pleasant sleigh type ride leading to the labor intensive work ahead. We would sometimes carry extra hay as a snack for the cattle. There were signs that deer often congregated in this place and we saw their tracks all about the wood yard. When the snow was deep and the winter was tough, the deer would eat the freshly cut tree brush down to the size of a pencil. We would often leave hay for them to snack on during those harsh wintry conditions.

One of the special treats from that time of my life, which I've found impossible to duplicate as an adult, is the lunch we enjoyed on those days amidst a frozen, wooded landscape. It was common place to stop for a bite to eat sometime around mid day. This was a time of peace and quiet. Chain saws sat idle during our lunch with only the sound of a slight tick, tick, tick as their mufflers rapidly cooled.

The oxen were fed first. Caring for the animals is priority on a farm. In the frigid stillness, the cattle could be heard munching contentedly as we opened the brown bags holding our own lunches, unwrapping sandwiches lovingly prepared earlier that day by my mother.

As I sat beside my father on the dray of the scoot he used,

J. Adams
Edgecomb, ME

the treat I savored was two-fold. First were the frozen peanut butter and fluff sandwiches. It seems difficult to explain why they were so good or why their mere existence has stuck in my mind so clearly. It could have been because the fluff was stiff from its day in a paper sack during sub zero temperatures. When a frozen fluff sandwich is removed from a plastic bag it is not messy and is much easier to eat. Added to this was the thermos full of hot chocolate. The cocoa was incredibly hot coming out of that thermos, making it a necessity to set our filled cups into the snow in order to cool it down enough to drink. The rich, chocolaty liquid was an exceptional treat on those bitter days. Even more special was the opportunity to drink from the thermos my dad carried to work. I have always respected and admired my father. Sharing that thermos with him on those days of hard work made me feel important, grownup, capable and responsible.

Those days are long past and I rarely drive oxen anymore. I heat my home with wood but the majority are wood pellets, made in Maine and purchased locally.

Although I've not been able to duplicate that frozen peanut butter and fluff sandwich, I have bought a Stanley thermos for my own use. During long winter hikes on a mountain trail, I carry it in my backpack. I cherish those moments when, after pouring a cup of steaming hot chocolate, I can close my eyes and listen for the ticking of a cooling chainsaw muffler while imagining a pair of Red Durhams munching hay behind me.

Oh, the things you never realize you'll miss until they are gone!

W.R. Olsen
South Bristol, ME

Better Life

I was born in Brooklyn, New York, the fifth child of a Laplander mother who never did master the English language and a Norwegian sea-faring man. Most of my friends were first generation Americans. That was what Brooklyn was made up of. My parents are buried there. But their children moved on. I loved the country of my parents' choosing. Patriotism was like breathing, so naturally I enlisted to serve our country.

After the service the search to better locate myself in life found me in a nice suburban town, a prosperous business, but I also found in myself another person. I discovered a materialist! I found a person who was not real, not caring. This person was living in what he thought was the "great American way." He was going to retire by forty, work hard but still be able to vacation a couple of months a year at his summer home in Maine. Not caring who he cut off or put down in the rush for "the better life." I remember looking back at that "better life"—in the recovery room—If it was so good, how come that box was sitting there, with the wire coming out of it and into a hole in my chest?

Daniel Jamieson
Candler, NC

From Upper Hominy Valley

Spring births in a burst of solar energy—
Festive confetti ascends the deciduous slopes of
    Mount Pisgah
To its summit, to an iron steeple pointing out to infinity
transmitting man's inessential votives to a deaf and dumb
    universe.
How can they not know that the *answer* is here:
    Here is the rebirth of ever-returning seasons,
    Here in our *'land of the sky'*
      Behold:
Breathe our sweet air: fecund, fertile fields respond daily
growing from man's labors, his needs, until the end of time
when our living planet is burned out and becomes solar
    dust
billowing like *Sirius* clouds in a void where there is no *time.*
    Surely you cannot expect any other response from
    infinity,
        Could you?

Steve Troyanovich
Florence, NJ

softly...in wingless dream
for Elizabeth

*darkness unfolds its starry wings
and flies away with a nameless world*
—Erik Lindegren

once upon my dream
i touched you.
your eyes gave me
both ends of a rainbow.
in the early dawn wind
i felt your abandonment
nowhere was warm...
memory remains
hiding behind
your smile

***

Thomas C. Collins
New Harbor, ME

When to Write Poetry—A List

1. When bored.

2. When enthused.

3. When awakened from a bad dream.

4. When inspiration strikes.

5. When exercising your mind.

And other times deemed appropriate.

Goose River Anthology, 2013//165

Peggy Trojan
Brule, WI

Last Stage
for Dar

Your death no longer
stabs me
in staccato surprises,
catching me
unprepared for
crying in the street.
No longer startles.
The sharpness
is rounding,
as knives dull with use.

I have lived all
the stages you died.
Denial, anger,
and the letting go.

It is even easy now
to let you come walking
soft like wonder
through my mind.

Susan Connelly
St. George, ME

Sweet Airs

Be not afeared: the isle is full of noises,
Sounds and sweet airs that give delight and hurt not.
                                        The Tempest

A dozen years of life's sea changes, a new century, and I am on my way, this time alone, to a place of shared memories.

Labor Day weekend. North from Massachusetts, through New Hampshire, slowing for the tolls at Portsmouth. Behind me, a few cars wait to pay and be on their way. The southbound lanes are jammed with cars heading for where I just came from.

Familiar sights appear. A pottery shop, a little painted wagon with customers lined up for lobster rolls. That square house, colored a rich lilac, used to be black. The asters and Queen Anne's Lace are in fuller bloom than at home.

It has been a quarter century since I first met the local innkeeper. He wears the years well—few lines on his round face, light hair just beginning to gray. "Just one night?" he says, turning the guest log toward me. "That's too bad."

I go for a walk in the cool evening and pass a small market that sells live lobsters. The gas pump in front is so antiquated that the price of gas is shown as $1.60. A Post-it next to "Total Sale" instructs: "Please double." There is the modern school building, just down the street from the site of a 19th century academy for young ladies. The Ladies Aid chowder supper will begin at 5 P.M.

The library on the first floor of the inn offers a complete Shakespeare and a complete Poe. I pass on both in favor of the Nebula awards, which I take back to my room and read cover to cover.

In the morning, the harbor is as still as a painting. I sit

Susan Connelly
St. George, ME

by the dining room windows admiring the view, entertained by the way guests quickly revise their breakfast orders upon learning that breakfast is included in the room rate. I fetch my car from under the chestnut trees and head east toward the regional airport. After all this time—after 9/11—it's still easy. I write a check, hand my sleeping bag and boxes to the pilot, and in minutes we leave the ground.

And in less than a quarter hour, we are coming down over the island. I see Henry waiting in the tall grass, and wonder how the years will have changed him. Helping me down the plane steps he looks much the same, tanned and freckled, in a blue shirt, chinos and scruffy moccasins. I see that the red hair he passed on to his children and grandchildren is long and white.

Maps show the island's main road as "Unimproved Dirt." Salt, wind, and water have stripped the paint from most of the houses and from the lobster boat still listing in the yard where I first saw it.

Down the last path to the A-frame. Someone—Henry, perhaps, or one of his children—has made improvements to the house. A new outhouse, and screens to replace the ones that let in Maine-sized mosquitoes. A propane stove in which I will make baking powder biscuits. A high, firm, comfortable couch. And on the draining board, a pale green mug, evidently not as fragile as it always looked, sits on a thin towel with a faded pattern of roses.

One improvement I wasn't expecting was a phone. And a large silver radio hogging space on the table. As soon as I am alone I unplug them both and stash them out of sight in a cupboard that holds games and jigsaw puzzles.

On my first walk, the tide is out. Its cold, briny smell follows me to the little cemetery. Most of the islanders who died in the last twelve years were Henry's age, but there is the name of the woman who lived off to the east and grew wonderful vegetables and berries. I see by the carved dates that she was older than I thought.

Susan Connelly
St. George, ME

I walk back, turn on some lights and make dinner. I can hear the ocean, and the throbbing engines of the last lobster boats returning before dark. I read the soggy *New Yorkers* (practically current—2003, filled with articles on the presidential campaign). I take a book upstairs, read for a while in the deep quiet, and sleep wonderfully until daylight comes through the yellow and black checked curtains.

I establish a routine that I will follow for the ensuing week of fine weather. Coffee and a book in bed, the open windows bringing a breeze from two directions. The outdoor shower, with the wind blowing the curtain and carrying the smell of the sea. Breakfast, then a walk to the landing strip, where on different days I will see Bobolinks, Horned Larks and a Scarlet Tanager. Most mornings, I pass an old man watering giant nasturtiums he has planted by the side of the road.

Back at the A-frame, I make a second cup of coffee and drink it on the deck, where the sun is September warm. Then it is time for my morning study, accompanied by a tall, iced glass of the island's sweet water. Homer, read aloud to the sound of the *much-foaming* sea. Juvenal, portraying a Rome as decadent, corrupt and uninhabitable as any modern city. After lunch, I walk to the harbor and on to the gravelly beach at the island's north end. The afternoon is for sewing quilt squares and translating Suetonius's *Life of Virgil*. I have a luxury the great epic poet was denied—I can toss unsatisfactory drafts into the woodstove.

My last walk of the day is along the southern cliffs and the length of the beach, then east past the house of the woman I didn't expect to find in the cemetery. The graveyard itself looks peaceful in the golden light. By the time I get back to the house, the first stars have appeared.

On Wednesday, I arrive at the airstrip just in time to see the plane coming in. It takes on a passenger and taxis south to the edge of the asters, turns and rolls north, and lifts into the sky like one of the brown summer grasshoppers.

Susan Connelly
St. George, ME

On my way back I encounter Henry, who stops his truck in the middle of the road to invite me to High Tea. This is island talk for using up the last of your food before leaving for home. I accept, and at 5 P.M. am walking past a glory of fall flowers and knocking on the side door. Henry has me sit where the view is best, and sets out cheddar, goat cheese dip, carrots, celery, and crackers softened by the moist air. He has made tea, but alerts me that the milk has gone bad.

Henry is going to be taking the plane back with me on Saturday. We say good-bye until then and I walk back under a black sky filled with stars.

Friday comes and I take a last walk to see the sky over the beach turning pale blue in the hour before sunset. I pack, tidy the A-frame, and before going to bed walk out on the deck for one more look at the constellations. There is Orion, harbinger of winter.

Saturday morning Henry comes rattling down the path. He offers to take a photo of me with my coffee and *Twelfth Night,* but the illusion of having spent a week in which twenty-five years have vanished is near perfect. I need no camera to remind me that I am now the same age Henry was in 1980.

We wave to everybody along the way and Henry expounds on the subject of Island Cars. "Stage three," he says, "is when the fuel pump goes, and you put a gas can on a stick, run a hose, and let gravity feed the carburetor." He urges me to retire my own car to an island, but at 30,000 miles, it has a way to go before it is eligible.

On the airstrip, somebody is walking a dog. Henry speaks to him, and the man gets off the runway just as we hear the plane approaching. Henry says to me, "When the wind is out of the North, he has to clear that barn and come in over the trees. He can't see the runway until he's almost on it. If somebody's on the airstrip, he doesn't have a lot of options. It's either hit the jogger or crush the goldenrod."

Henry sits up front to "get a few pointers" from the pilot. The ruby-red "check engine" light doesn't go out as the pro-

Susan Connelly
St. George, ME

peller starts to turn; and the pilot looks in the mirror at me and covers it with a Post-it. The woman next to me wants to take pictures, so the pilot circles the island at a low altitude. I see all the sights I have been enjoying for a week, then we are back at the airstrip and the plane is climbing into the cloudless sky.

At the airport I claim my car (long-term parking is a dollar a day), and start it up with the unfamiliar-feeling key. Henry helps load my luggage, including the trash I will take back to Massachusetts, and I say goodbye to him. At the end of the airport drive I turn left, and there is civilization. Cars, people, anything and everything to buy. But I need no souvenir of my sublime week. I turn right onto a road that will take me to Route One, and am passed by a car with a vanity plate in Latin. CUR NON.

Next year. *Why not?*

***

Thomas Peter Bennett
Bradenton, FL

No Return

In time and space,
flights and lives,
have points of
     no return.

Beth Ellen Jack
Lake Forest, CA

Waiting for a Hummingbird
Dedicated to Benjamin Thomas Sharp
(my second dad)

Do specific words bring comfort
like waiting for the same humming bird
to return each summer, yet knowing
he may dart away with a burst of color;
or do we recognizing past conversations
can echo and linger
like drills of the wood-pecker,
who resonates a bold Morse-code
we have yet to decipher;

we cannot postpone that pull of gravity,
or pain of grief that shapes hard objects
like water to stone; appearances shift
like Miro sculptures, suddenly unfamiliar,
but love succeeds and remains with us;
just as hilltops whiten in moonlight,
jasmine drapes like scented chandeliers,
dampness spreads among the magnolias
and solitude reigns like hooded owls
among the shadows; love exists like a signature;

love overlaps with where he sat or laughed,
from outdoor concerts, picnics, favorite lyrics,
novelists discussed, family meals, covered bridges,
pebbles in a stream, rises with loons calling,
humming of locusts at dusk, lighthouse in the fog,
thoughts of him flower inside us;
when melancholy repeats like a distant train whistle,

(continued)

Beth Ellen Jack
Lake Forest, CA

fading into darkness, our commitment of memory
    transfigures,
love triumphs, just as barren fields yield new growth,
and we once bent over like scarecrows,
can stand up like majestic oaks.

love flourishes with the hyacinth, who refuses
to mourn her purple, until we are ready for new blooms
to grace our cognitive gardens, every space reminiscent
of his presence, that Virginia drawl,
Southern hospitality and warmth of the hearth;
how his ideas and opinions held truth
like amber beads under glass and pure.

***

Robert B. Moreland
Pleasant Prairie, WI

Keno Drive-in

Summer's end, as a double feature plays
we cuddle in Dad's borrowed Chevrolet
munching the last of the pretzels as you,
my girl, use my shoulder as your pillow.
Ending inevitable, right triumphs
as the hero targets the vile villain!
Cotton candy lost during a stolen kiss
acts like flypaper tacking your gingham
down on the faded blue cloth upholstery.
Soon, autumn's chill will try to erase
these summer memories. But not tonight.

Irene Zimmerman
Milwaukee, WI

Resurrection

My mother died eight years ago today.
Late this afternoon I picked my way
through a new-plowed field to a path in a greening woods
where flowers had pushed through winter leaves and stones
to tell a parable of life and death.

I heard the earth beneath me hold its breath
and felt my mother's rhythms in my bones—
a symphony of pathed and unpathed woods,
of Beethoven and books—strange, lovely blend
of careful and uncultivated ways—
and realized her life will never end.

The dead have powers
to roll away the stones of earth and hours,
to burst through bonds of unplowed space and time,
and sign their presence with perennial flowers.

Dwayne Magee
Mechanicsburg, PA

Lost in Thailand

Bangkok, Thailand is about as far away from my house as I can get without starting to come back again. For me, it is literally on the opposite side of Earth. My grueling journey across our expansive planet in 1986 took me over 8,000 miles by plane from my home. The flight was made even more unpleasant when, somewhere over the Pacific, the woman sitting next to me regurgitated her breakfast into a warm, soupy mix onto the floor around my feet. As the malodorous conglomeration of undigested bacon and orange juice crept toward my stowed away carryon bag, I longed for nothing more than to be seated in the nose of the aircraft with the crew.

You see, for me, the hardest part about flying is not the discomfort of being forcibly confined into an appointed space with strangers brandishing their disagreeable habits and smells. For me, the hardest part about flying is the necessity of putting my trust in the nameless, faceless individuals flying the plane. It is the pilot who ultimately has the responsibility of locating and successfully transporting me to my destination, and pilots tend to say remarkably very little to their passengers while they are flying, even on an 18 hour flight. As such, my mind begins to wonder. How am I supposed to know if we are even flying in the right direction? I want the pilot to explain to me over the loudspeaker where Thailand is and how it is we are going to find it. Thailand is only the 51st largest country by total area in the world. It's not like trying to land in Canada. Who couldn't hit that?

Our pilot spoke only twice throughout our entire flight. The first time he said, "Hey, Joe. Is this thing on?" and then we heard a click. Then, a few hours later he said, "Hey, Joe. Did someone just throw up back there? I'm sure glad I'm not that guy sitting next to her! Hey. Wait a minute. Is this thing

Dwayne Magee
Mechanicsburg, PA

on again?" and then we heard another click.

Flying to Bangkok turned out to be less of an ordeal than driving in Bangkok. An organization called *The Global Road Safety Partnership* reports that, in terms of road-crash deaths and injuries, Thailand ranks among the top ten in the world with more than 1,000 fatalities per month and roughly 80,000 injuries per year. Every day, the streets are filled with tens of thousands of automobiles, heavy trucks, three-wheeled tuk-tuks, and overcrowded buses. On my trip from the airport, I saw motorcycles carrying entire families including new born babies, grandmothers, and family pets. Each family appeared to have only one helmet to share between them. Some slower automobile drivers, apparently too pre-occupied to be worried about the fact that they were actually sharing the streets, were crawling through traffic from the sides of the streets. Meanwhile, faster drivers were zooming past me from every direction, flashing their headlights as a means of signaling me that they were in a hurry and they had no intention of slowing down or yielding.

Most Thai people have never even taken a driver's test. If there is a test, I have deduced that it must pretty much only involve verifying that the potential driver can demonstrate a pulse. Posted speed limits, traffic signals, road signs, and the painted lines separating lanes are clearly only in place for aesthetic purposes because no one pays any attention to them. One of the travel guides I read stated that, "Driving in Thailand is not for the faint of heart. If you are a timid driver, easily annoyed, or believe that rules should be obeyed, we recommend you take public transportation." I would also recommend pre-medicating.

My plan while in Bangkok was to stay with some missionary friends who hailed from my home church. Jack and Lisa Miller were living there on a work visa which Jack had secured as a mechanical engineer. They were just a few people among thousands who have been coming to Thailand for the last 700 years to share Christianity with little to no suc-

Dwayne Magee
Mechanicsburg, PA

cess. The first were the Portuguese who were initially received warmly in the early 1500's. A century and a half later, the government killed or expelled all of them and closed down the borders. In all of the time that has passed since, less than one percent of the mostly Buddhist population has embraced the Christian faith. My friends were facing an uphill battle and I had very little concern that my visit would stand in the way of any sudden revivals.

The morning after I arrived, things started off quite literally with a bang when Jack and Lisa's youngest son wondered out of the house, climbed into the family van, pulled it out of gear, and successfully coasted it out of the driveway into the front fender of a passing motorist. Jack had just finished explaining to me that the Thai language was a tonal language and it was sometimes difficult for him to understand. He said that even after three years in Bangkok he was still learning new words and some of Thai's more subtle nuances. As Jack rushed out of the house to retrieve his son, I noticed that the passing motorist whose car was just damaged was waving his arms and shouting. He was, no doubt, teaching Jack more new words and helping him with some of those aforementioned nuances.

Most Thai people have nicknames or play names (chuu len) as they call them. For instance, Jack's neighbor was called *Daeng* due to the reddish color of her skin when she was born. Other nicknames I learned while on my trip were: *Faa* (blue), *Yai* (big), *Moo* (pork), *Poo* (crab), and *Phung* (bee). These designations are usually chosen by family members and they stay with people their entire lives. Nicknames can be ascribed to individuals based upon looks, behaviors, or events. As I observed Jack's animated discourse with the inconsolable motorist amidst the wreckage at the end of his driveway, I wondered if Jack might be proudly acquiring his first Thai nickname.

After breakfast and the excitement of the accident, we all piled into Jack's newly dented vehicle and rushed off through

Dwayne Magee
Mechanicsburg, PA

the busy streets of Bangkok. I presumed that we were driv-
ing towards all of the conveniences of modern day commerce
to look for plastic souvenirs, experience some of the local,
spicy cuisine, and perhaps stop by a museum or two to learn
all about this breathtaking country, rich with history and
ancient temples but Jack had something completely different
in mind.

"When we get to the floating market," he announced, "try
to stick together. There will be a lot of people there and many
of them will want your money in a very bad way."

I dismissed (and soon regretted dismissing) Jack's warn-
ing in much the same way I have so often dismissed (and
similarly regretted) similar warnings from my mother.
Shortly after we parked and exited our vehicle, I wondered
ahead of our group. Within minutes, I found myself sporting
two giant, slithering pythons as necklaces while a very fast
speaking, picture taking, young Thai gentleman was
demanding 300 baht for the unflattering, mouth agape, eyes-
wide open, snapshot he had just taken of me.

A faint, gurgling noise that sounded very much like a
combination of *Errrr*! and *Help*!—"Eerrrrp!" was about all I
could muster as the two serpents bore down on my throat. I
desperately looked to Jack, who was just now arriving to the
scene. With watering eyes, I attempted to communicate to
him my deepest regret for not heading his admonition and
my very strong desire for him to pay the man whatever he
wanted as quickly as possible. Jack, having several years of
experience in matters related to buying and selling in
Bangkok, seemed to be in no hurry to facilitate my extrica-
tion. As I struggled for breath, he casually engaged the man
in a friendly, monetary negotiation for my release which,
when the matter was concluded, turned out to be a very dis-
appointing 1/3 of the original asking price.

"I would have thought I was worth more than that," I
sheepishly joked, softly elbowing Jack in the ribs as the color
returned to my face. Then, in an effort to quell Jack's grow-

Dwayne Magee
Mechanicsburg, PA

ing agitation with me I asked, "So, what is a floating market anyway?"

Jack glared at me for a moment and turned his lips inward as if to say, "Serves you right!" or "Next time, I'm leaving you at home!" But eventually he saw the whole episode as an opportunity to liven up his next, otherwise dull and repetitive, monthly missionary newsletter and his anger subsided. As we walked, he explained to me the critical role that rivers have played in the economic history of the Thai people.

"For hundreds and perhaps thousands of years," he said, "villagers have been buying, selling, and trading goods by boat on the vast system of natural waterways within the lush jungles that blanket over one fourth of the country's landscape."

He further explained that for convenience, many bodies of water were eventually connected to each other through the construction of canals called klongs. Over time, the maze of rivers throughout the countryside grew intricate and complicated.

"You wouldn't want to attempt to navigate these waters without an experienced guide," he warned. "One wrong turn and you would never be heard from again."

I thought back to my prior mistake which had resulted in my sudden adornment of an ophidian necklace. I pictured myself standing in a boat somewhere in the middle of a river in the dense, Thai jungle, scratching my head wondering whether or not I should have turned left or right at that last fork in the river.

"I'll just follow you then," I replied meekly.

The Ratchaburi floating market resides in one of the largest systems of klongs in Thailand. It is the *King* Klong, if you will. Thousands of people come from far and wide each day to barter and trade fresh, tropical produce, flowers, vegetables, and hand crafted goods. The unique experience of shopping by boat is captivating, especially when you consider the fact that there are no stores. All transactions take

Dwayne Magee
Mechanicsburg, PA

place vessel-to-vessel as patrons and merchants float along-side of each other in a never-ending, liquid plaza.

We walked on until we came to a series of elevated, wooden sidewalks that reminded me of the boardwalks and piers along the beaches of the Atlantic back home. The walkways were poorly constructed and partially covered with rusted metal and bamboo. These makeshift structures stretched on for hundreds of yards in both directions and on both sides of a murky, brown river. The river was densely populated with small, aging boats piloted by small, aging women. There were so many boats I could have easily walked across the river without getting my feet wet. Some of the boats were filled with fat, American tourists while others belonged to Thai merchants who were cargoing straw hats, Malacca grapes, Chinese grapefruits, mangoes, bananas, coconuts, colorful umbrellas, wood carvings, souvenir Buddha's and countless other things. Somewhere nearby someone was cooking something and the smell of meat and sweat filled my nostrils. I found myself fending off unpleasant memories of the aerial voyage that brought me here the night before.

Jack adeptly negotiated a fee for our nautical excursion and we climbed into a wooden, long-tailed boat operated by a Thai woman who appeared to be roughly the age of my grandmother's grandmother. I looked at Jack with my best, "Are you kidding me?" eyes but he gave me the *thumbs* up sign and told me not to worry. Seeing that there were no life jackets, I found my seat and with that, we were on our way.

About an hour into our excursion, after we had purchased some fresh pineapple, two straw hats and a small, hand carved wooden stool, Jack paid our elderly boat captain 500 baht (about $20.00) to take us away from the crowds and into the country side. "I think it is important that you get to see firsthand the places where these people live," he said. And then he added with a perceptible tone of uncertainty, "I am pretty sure it will be safe."

As we escaped through the outskirts of the floating city,

Dwayne Magee
Mechanicsburg, PA

the hustle and bustle of commerce faded into the distance behind us. The crowds of humanity dissipated and we were soon surrounded by thick, dark forests. We were drifting quietly, except for the gentle splash of the old woman's oars when an angry, wrinkled man suddenly appeared on the shore to our right as if he had been brought there by a bolt of lightning. He was short and thin; very thin. I could see his skeleton stirring under his brown, leathery skin as he shouted at us. His receding hair was long and silvery and it seemed to dance like white fire around the silhouette of his toothless skull. He wore ragged, khaki shorts and a sleeveless t-shirt which hung like ragged curtains on his malnourished form. If he had not been so fully animated in his conduct I would have taken him for the corpse of a recently departed, chain smoking, centenarian.

I do not understand one word of the Thai language (as was evident earlier that day when I inadvertently told Jack his driveway was delicious) but the man's tone and body language clearly articulated desperate agitation. He seemed to me to be saying something on the order of, "Go back to where you came from you deplorable beasts" and "May sickness and disease come upon you and your families for generations to come so that any memory of you is wiped away from this cursed planet forever!"

"What's he saying?" I asked Jack.

"I'm not sure," Jack lied. "I think he is admiring our pineapples."

Jack slipped our tour guide another 500 baht and whispered to her something in Thai that I will forever interpret to be the Thai equivalent to the American phrase, "Step on it!" With that, the old woman's newly inspired arms paddled us vigorously past the ill-tempered, rattling sack of bones until we were well out of sight and much further down river.

The National Research Council divides Thailand into six geographical regions: North, Northeast, East, South, Central, and West. The regions supposedly differ from each other in

Dwayne Magee
Mechanicsburg, PA

many ways including population and social and economic development. But where we were, near Bangkok in the central region, it appeared to me as though the regions might have converged. Our boat floated past dilapidated, wooden shacks where naked children with swollen bellies played outside and defecated into the same waters where their mothers were washing clothes and dishes. In the hills above them, a mere 50 or 60 yards away, stood gated, brick mansions with balconies and swimming pools. The water from their elevated, well-groomed lawns was no doubt seeping its way through the ground and down below, into the drinking cups of the poverty-stricken masses below them. We were now about an hour away from the busiest floating market in Thailand and I wondered how many tourists had never seen what I was seeing.

The jungle around us was also full of diversity and disparity. Thailand is home to 1,500 different kinds of trees, 800 types of ferns, 176 kinds of snakes, 925 kinds of birds, and 282 animal species. It boasts 27,000 kinds of flowers including 1,300 different types of orchids. The high levels of annual rainfall and average temperatures that rarely fall below 70 degrees allow Thailand's ecosystem to be one of the most productive in the world. I felt like Dorothy must have felt in *The Wizard of Oz* when she opened the door of her black and white bedroom into the colorful world of Oz.

We paddled on for another hour or two, turning right and left, and every which way as the rivers and streams broke apart into more rivers and streams. Eventually, the boat traffic around us began to pick up a little and we soon found ourselves drifting into another wretched and impoverished population center. I was starting to feel overcome with sadness in the midst of the infinite need surrounding us when, as if brought there on another bolt of lightning, the angry, cursing old man from up river reappeared on the bank of the river again, near our drifting vessel.

"That's impossible!" Jack exclaimed. "How did he get

Dwayne Magee
Mechanicsburg, PA

here?"

Vinyan! ("Evil Spirit!") The old woman in our boat exclaimed.

I was inclined to agree. There could be no natural, rational explanation for his reappearance. He was either a ghost or he was someone with access to a time portal. We were miles from where we last saw him and the only way here was by boat or by helicopter. He could not have been someone with the means for either.

As he barraged us again with more of his angry curses, I grew less frightened and more sympathetic. I was sorry for him and for all those around us who were so irredeemably immersed in endless poverty. The Thai people perceive the world to be riddled with ghosts and evil spirits but this man was only a lost soul living in a world of impossible destitution. I suddenly found myself feeling very thankful for people like Jack and Lisa.

I came to Thailand to see golden palaces, beautiful Thai dancers, and restaurants so big that the waitresses moved about on roller skates. I came to take morning strolls through exquisite gardens with unfathomable views of brilliant sunsets and stunning waterfalls. I came to visit my friends, the missionaries. I saw everything I wanted to see and more. I saw everything I wanted to see and less. I saw what it truly means to be lost.

Ann M. Penton
Green Valley, AZ

Hard Times on the Soft Felt

In the corporate pool game
you get hugs twice—
once in that big triangular group huddle
when you've been invited to start their game,
and the second from a few caring colleagues
who happen to still be in the vicinity
of the corner pocket
where you exit.

In between, there's a lot of alone time
interspersed with the taking of many hits,
getting knocked in unexpected directions,
bouncing off walls.

***

Mayflower Society:
The Extended Family

Unless drastic circumstances befell them,
the Mayflower's Old English Mastiff
and Springer Spaniel,
and some of the ship's mousers as well,
by now most likely each have bevies
of New World descendants, too—
plus all the progeny
of any disembarked mice.

Sherry Ballou Hanson
Brunswick, ME

Body Search

In sunlight the promise of spring
but still a cold bite to the wind,
Coast Guard sweep for a fisherman
gone missing from his boat at sea.

Channel 8 news crew smoking and filming,
sea plane flying a grid overhead,
chopper hovering above.

I'm huddled among slabs of sparkling granite
wondering if the sea will give him up
this day, or maybe not.
He's someone's son, husband, father
making his living on the water
and a cold grave at sea is the worst
for those waiting hour to hour.

**

P. C. Moorehead
North Lake, WI

Climbing

This is a dark mountain we climb,
gloomy and old.
I look at my feet.
A blossom appears.

Hannah Fox Trowbridge
Harpswell, ME

Hard to Believe

Hilarious are the tales amongst
the older crowd. "Can't remember"
is the latest past-time game. It generates
endless stories. Where were we going?
I forgot my best friend's name! You
look familiar, but who are you? I baked
a batch of cookies—
can't remember who they're for!

When kept a secret,
this forgetting thing can get scary.
But shared, there is a great variety,
as each story tries to outdo the next.
Each one keeps the hilarity coming.

***

Steve Troyanovich
Florence, NJ

for Rabindranath Tagore

i watch the snowflakes
peacefully caress this earth
and ask: where is the other
peace?

Hannah Fox Trowbridge
Harpswell, ME

My Ocean

Immersed and swimming for pleasure and or exercise in the salt water that is the just-right temperature wasn't in itself an unusual thing for me. But unexpectedly one day, my skin's sensation of the warm ocean water enveloping me was that of liquid satin, a soft caressing of every inch of me. During the summer, I often walked across our field and down to the shore, a short distance of a few hundred yards. Our moderately-sized cove is a bit rocky, just big enough to launch a couple of kayaks and to hold a bunch of people to have a swim. It's well protected from the open ocean, yet benefits from the Gulf Stream that flows past every year. Most people I know avoid the cold water, even when I tell them about the summer's Gulf Stream that always visits for a few weeks.

I never expected anything different that day when I easily walked in. No cold or sharp intake of breath, just an easy step by deeper step in, followed by an easy submersion dive. The salty aroma of the beach, seaweed and water is always almost as enticing to my nostrils and breath as that of freshly baked bread and invariably draws me to immerse myself into the source.

When I came up for my first breath, I could hardly believe what I felt, being surrounded as I was, like in an ocean womb. I'd been feeling sad for a while. I'd scattered some of my daughter Susan's ashes in the cove two years earlier. Swimming in the cove used to be a favorite thing for her. The ocean water was literally holding me, holding me up. It felt like a forever kind of thing. I floated with my eyes closed and let the water be like a satin second skin. The earth seemed to be turning me around counter clock-wise until I opened my eyes and discovered I wasn't turning at all. I was floating in the same direction as before. Each time I closed my

Hannah Fox Trowbridge
Harpswell, ME

eyes, the earth seemed to turn me like that until I opened them again. I didn't know which sensation I preferred, but it didn't matter. Being held by the earth's oceans—they are all connected—felt to me like my body was the ocean. Literally, I almost was, being ninety-eight percent water, salt water. So I could let myself go and be just that. Me, the ocean was floating and turning inside itself.

I wanted to stay there in that physical, emotional and spiritual place forever, so I did just that with a suspended time warp sort of sensation. I felt closer to Susan, too. But of course, the ocean was warm but not warm enough at sixty-eight degrees for me to stay there for a really long time. I eventually chilled and finally had to reluctantly return to my land-based body.

It was a peak experience I had that day. Though I have swum there many times since, I have only repeated it very partially a few fragmented times since then and have never fully recaptured that emersion experience. I think I'll always remember the satiny ocean support sensation that held me so lovingly that day. No human touch that I can imagine could ever match it.

***

Thomas Peter Bennett
Bradenton, FL

Airport

Waiting.
Waiting.
Waiting.

Maude Olsen
South Bristol, ME

Family

I grew up in a family in which a human body was regard-ed as a perfectly normal thing to have. It was not something to exploit, misuse, make fun of, or necessarily hide. Everyone had one and they came in all different colors, shapes, and sizes, according to one's ancestry...or God's whim.

As we moved every couple of years, following Dad's sta-tion of service (U.S. Navy), we saw a pretty complete sampling of the world's population, thereby making us prone to accepting whatever the norm where we were living at the time. It wasn't long before one realized that no matter what the package looked like, the insides were apt to be very sim-ilar. Feelings, thoughts, ideas, and reactions might differ just enough to keep life interesting, yet confirm that we were all part of a large family, the family of human life on this planet.

***

Lorelee L. Sienkowski
Packwaukee, WI

Spring

Needles pierce fabric
creating a new design.
Green shoots pierce fresh earth.

Thomas Peter Bennett
Bradenton, FL

Snowbird

I didn't recognize you
in unfamiliar plumes,
as you swam near the dock,
until your body arched,
and in a graceful dive,
you sliced the water, and
then abruptly bobbed up.
　　Welcome neighbor, loon!
Like you, I wear Florida garb,
and enjoy the warm waters,
with fish for every meal.

***

January Hike

Accu Weather declares:
Very windy, snow,
if you were there;
Sunshine, breezy and humid,
since you are here.
With Maine a memory, and a
salubrious breeze at your back,
hike on in Florida.

Juliana L'Heureux
Topsham, ME

Media Pronunciation Alert:
Get Those Maine Names Right!

"La grammaire, qui sait régenter jusqu'aux aux rois."
—Moliere (1622-1673)
(To grammar, even kings must bow.)

Kennebunkport, Maine is a perfectly gorgeous place. It's visually compelling, especially when glamorous newscasters posture in front of the pristine Atlantic Ocean, a focal point in a coastal panorama, while reporting the political condition of our planet, often from the Bush compound at Walker's Point.

"Reporting live from Kenne-a-bunkport." Oh, no, not again!

Please, say it right!

Listening to the mispronounced names of beautiful Maine places is aggravating. It's as irritating as hearing your own name repeatedly stumbled over (like L'Heureux, for example!).

Miscued newscasters and pundits must think they sound freshly local or nouveau suave when they incorrectly pronounce some of Maine's beautiful locations. Sometimes, media folk from away even sound like they're trying to re-educate the locals about how to pronounce familiar names of places they're reporting about.

They act like the locals don't know how to talk.

Frankly, I'm weary of hearing Kennebunkport pronounced like someplace I've never been. For some reason, the correct pronunciation of this coastal town is frequently slurred by newscasters. Correctly pronounced, phonetically, it's "Ken-knee-bunk—port." Remember, to quickly slur the name's four syllables together. Practice saying it, all in one breath, like "Kenn*eeee*bunkport."

But, please, don't say "Kenn-A-bunk-port," (short "a") as

Juliana L'Heureux
Topsham, ME

though we locals don't know how to pronounce the name adopted by the town in 1821, when it was as a boat building site along the Kennebunk River.

Mispronouncing Kennebunkport is particularly irritating to the locals living in nearby Southern Maine towns. Some people think of this area as the 51st state in the Union, because it's not Massachusetts, yet more cosmopolitan than most of Maine.

By not pronouncing Kennebunkport correctly, the mistake has an unintended effect of causing the mispronunciation of the Town of Kennebunk and Kennebunk Beach, not be confused with their adjacent and more newsworthy and coastal neighbor.

Another frequent mispronunciation is Bangor, often slurred as "Bang-er." This amiable city is the county seat of Maine's Penobscot County, also known as the state's "Queen City of the East," although the reason it boasts this particular nickname is obscure. Nevertheless, the city's name is correctly pronounced "Bang-ORE," with the emphasis on the "ore," like "iron *ore.*" Unfortunately, some cable news weather forecasters find it oddly quaint to report dramatic blizzards forming in a place called "Bang-er," which doesn't exist. Those who mispronounce Bangor sound like they're sipping tea at high noon with their little pinky finger up, looking and sounding ridiculous.

Bangor is too stately a city to endure mispronunciations, because, after all, it's the historic birthplace of the iconic American fictional logger and folk hero, Paul Bunyan.

Let's also learn to correctly pronounce "Aroostook."

This special Maine place is lovingly called "The County." It's the largest acreage in one county east of the Mississippi River. There's a historic significance to The County, because it's home to thousands of the descendents of French Canadian settlers who populated the area before 1820, when Maine became a state. Many of these settlers were the refugees from the King Philip's War (1675-78) and the French

Juliana L'Heureux
Topsham, ME

and Indian Wars, waged in New England and Canada, including the victims of Le Grand Derangement, or "the expulsion" of the Acadians, in Grand Pre, Nova Scotia (the French colony of Acadia). Others migrated to the area from Quebec.

A benign international conflagration between the United States and Canada, called the Aroostook War of 1838-39, was a standoff waged in the area, without casualties. Fortunately, the incident eventually led to the signing of the Webster-Asburton Treaty, on August 9, 1842, when the definitive international border was established between Maine, Quebec, and New Brunswick, Canada.

But, The County's real name isn't pronounced "Aroostook" (like it is spelled). Rather, the correct phonetic pronunciation is "Aroost-uk," as though it's wrongly spelled.

Media geeks, tourists and grammarians alert! Kindly practice saying: "Kenn-*knee*-bunk-port," "Bang-*ore*" and "Aroost-uk." Okay?

Pronunciations notwithstanding, Mainers from all places, mispronounced, nicknamed, or otherwise—welcome tourists along with media folks, historians, natural beauty seekers and linguistics. Visitors from every cultural persuasion are encouraged to enjoy Maine's numerous attractions in scenic towns, cities, mountains, lakes, islands and wildlife, while experiencing the state's seasonal stages of magnificent natural beauty.

Of course, locals are impressed by the visitors who talk right. They make a wicked good impression.

Julia Ridge
Portland, ME

Number 17

Your graying hair, the asymmetry of your face, your
hammertoe, and the sneaker that made space for it—
a space still holding shape in a box in my house.

*Alone on your floor with a stricken heart: "Lie still, lie still
. . . breaking heart."*[*]

We poured what remained of your dust and bone into a
small white Tupperware box I found in the cupboard of
your kitchen; and

I lowered the box into the LL Bean tote you carried
everywhere. You used the box, then we used the box; and

Grim-faced, we walked through the streets of the town
where we lived once, and we bore the tote with you deep
down in it and draped in one of my sweaters.

*The soft sweet fragrance of pine bark filled September's air,
and dry leaves burned like incense as we passed by.*

LikeGoodSoldiers, we trod along. Mike leading. Tom and I
following—keeping pace. We climbed the crumbling granite
steps of St. Mary's to touch the painted doors.

We held paint chips in our hands like relics, wondering
what, if anything, we understood; we ambled past the
movie theatre and soda shop where Mike always met his
friends.

Julia Ridge
Portland, ME

We peeked inside windows at the high school like ghost
lingerers of a forgotten past; and we sat on a picnic table at
Roland Green Elementary, as if the bell just rang.

ThisWeDidWithOurEyesClosed, we said. We headed home
past Findlay's Market and the house on the corner of South
Main and Spring, and we walked atop its stony wall;

We went up Aspen Street and passed the Van's, along
Smiley Avenue and passed the woods thinned by
development.

Then we turned right on to Beech Street and walked down
to Number 17 on the left.

All these years later we stood in front of the house we'd
fled; and the owner invited us in; and Tom and Mike
accepted.

*And I poured you, Ma, from the plastic box and felt your
dusty cells upon my hand. And I watched as your ashes fell
between the sidewalk and the lawn. And I watched as they
settled along the edges, Ma, where you were "happiest"
once.*

[*]Thank you to Christina Rossetti for the phrase,
"lie still . . . breaking heart" from the poem *Mirage*.

Patrick T. Randolph
Kalamazoo, MI

The Simple Surprise

The heater kicks on at two in the morning,
You turn in bed and come closer.

My eyes open to a strange light-darkness,
It's snowing outside—no wind.

Your left leg is warm—almost hot.
My fingers search and find your fingers.

I squeeze them and wait—you return
A strong squeeze, then soft laughter;

You've been awake now for an hour—
And tell me I've been snoring a song.

***

Compassion

Dodging ants,

Morning walk—

Humbled, I grin.

Kathy McHugh
Ogunquit, ME

Camp Memories

It was a long and dreaded two hour ride to the camp in the White Mountains where my family and I spent most weekends and vacations as I grew up. I often wonder how my life would have been without having spent so much time up there, so isolated, with one friend and few neighbors. I made the most of it yet wished to be elsewhere. But it is sad that our camp may have been destroyed during Hurricane Irene, when the forty foot wide Mad River expanded to one hundred feet, ravaging the area of New Hampshire Route 49.

My creativity was stretched to the limits. I named rocks in the river, held a funeral for a mouse, listened to my brother play guitar, put together the same puzzle which had a missing piece, and pretended I was in commercials for soap and cosmetics. If my friend Dianne was there we talked, laughed and read comics. We toasted marshmallows and told stories by the fire. We played horse shoes, piled wood, fished, went hiking and got lost in the woods, fed cows at the farm, filled water jugs at the spring and watched my dad take photos of chipmunks and mushrooms.

Dad, Gerry Ahern, and Whirley Jackson bought land in Waterville Valley from a farmer named Gilman. We started off in tents, graduating to an eight by ten screen utility house. By 1963 Dad had built a twenty-four by forty-eight foot cabin made of two thousand feet of cedar lumber from a large dismantled New England barn. This became our second home as well as Dad's get-away from his job at the phone company. We always slept well due to all the fresh air fluffing up the leaves and the loud rushing sound of the Mad River. Dad barbecued chicken, cut down trees and built dams. He constructed a twenty foot chimney with a four by ten one foot thick foundation, four hundred cement blocks lined with river stone inside and out, as well as a twenty-four foot deck

Kathy McHugh
Ogunquit, ME

we could fly-fish from. The Aherns built a similar cabin on the up-river side of his land and the Jacksons built an A-frame.

Winter weekends were especially tough. We wore snow-suits and snowshoes, shoveled out a place to park the car, then loaded up the toboggan with food and necessities and yanked it by rope down the 150 foot driveway. When we got inside it was so cold that we could see our breath. Dad lit the fire and heated rocks to warm our beds. He and my brother had to shovel snow off the roof so it wouldn't cave in.

Channel eight had country music shows, square dancing and humorous weather reports from the top of Mount Washington. We went to the Flume, the Polar Caves, and Ruggle's Mine. I especially enjoyed in the town of Plymouth a nearby teachers' college that had an excellent book store. We saw the foliage along the Kancamagus Highway. We attended the annual Labor Day bonfire at the Gilman's.

The radio operator of Dad's bomber crew and his family from West Virginia came up to visit, as did Reverend Joop who once wed Mom and Dad. Cousin Martha brought three dogs that chased me around the camp and tried to bite me. My grandfather came up for fishing weekends. One night he suddenly stopped snoring so my brother and I woke up our parents to make sure that he was okay. Another time teenagers broke in and stole sleeping bags, food and liquor. They were later found at the Campton Campground with bad hangovers.

My parents sold the camp when they retired in 1980. By then it had indoor plumbing, a dishwasher, washer, dryer and a twenty foot well. The adult Aherns and Jacksons have since passed away, but I did attend Mrs. Jackson's 100th birthday party. Although I vacation my way now, I hope the camp survived Hurricane Irene. It meant a lot to Dad, and so to all of us. He made it special. In my heart our camp on the Mad River will always be there. Maybe it wasn't so bad after all...

Charles Van Buren
Brunswick, GA

If I Could

We grew up together, you and I,
I thought of you as a brother,
I told you the innermost secrets,
that I would tell no other.

We laughed and played our days away,
thinking it would never change,
now looking back in retrospect,
the reasons seem so strange.

Whether we merely grew apart,
or the reasons were more sublime,
we didn't really talk that much,
for a very, very, long time.

There are many things I'd like to say,
if I could, to your face,
but I'll never have the chance,
for you've gone to a higher place.

Earl Weigelt
Winslow, ME

The Lovely Gloom

When a fog rolls in and wraps wraith's arms
around the Head, the cliffs and heath;

When the flats' chill promise adorns the air aboard the
     living mist
and blends aromas fleetingly 'twixt apples, balsams, red
     rose hips;

When the hulking spruces spread their wings in haunting
     black relief
and rear above the leaden ledge to shadow waters deep;

When seagulls jeer and herons croak and geese and seals
     groan
and sea-bells sound and fog horns blow and blueberry
     barrens moan;

It sinks its teeth into a man, it grips him firm and sure
and attends his dreams both day and night—

such is Downeast's allure!

Janet Leahy
New Berlin, WI

Placement Matters

I am one of 26
when we stand together
I am in the fifth position

Within the larger 26 I belong to an inner circle of 5
In this lineup I am the second
All five of us are overused
and very tired
You can't write a word without
one of us

In the inner circle I really wish
I was the third
She always gets to go first
She is slim and trim
and loves to slip in front of me
She keeps repeating her mantra
I before thee
I before thee
such a silly rule
and she forgets . . .
there are exceptions

Sylvia Little-Sweat
Wingate, NC

Quilting Bee

When at rest from other work
Mother cut and pieced plain
and printed rag-bag scraps
fitting them like stained glass
to catch the light, hold the dark.
Some agreed upon winter day
she laid the quilt top, batting,
lining between Grandma's
wooden frames to hang by
chains a table of layered cloth
for neighbors' restive hands
like flitting summer moths
to settle lightly on. Playing
at Mother's feet I could see
only laps and knees, random
hands reaching underneath
to trace magical fairy-dust
trails overhead. Quilting
from the center to the outer
edge, they sat on straight-back
kitchen chairs, their talk soft
as cotton candy at the County
Fair. Like signatures on family
documents, names they chose
to write in Bibles, those rows
of minute stitches—Timelines
neatly drawn that winter day—
would in time outlast them all.

Maggie Atwood
Newcastle, ME

Duet

Animals are much less intelligent than you are inclined to think, but in their feelings and emotions they are far less different from most of us than you assume. Geese, for instance, possess a veritably human capacity for grief.
—Conrad Lorenz

The goose was found with her long neck laid across her dead mate's body. He had been hit by a car earlier in the day and the goose had refused to leave her gander's side. She would not eat that evening. Over the next week her sadness was so great that she simply walked in circles, crying out with deafening honks, refusing all food.

Her owner decided that placing the goose with other waterfowl might increase her chances of survival so she brought her over to the river letting her loose by my house a short distance from the flock. I watched as the goose welcomed the water, making graceful turns to the left, then right, submerging her head and arching it back up so that the water ran down her neck in tiny streams. The flock watched but made no move toward her. Eventually she glided in their direction but was bitten repeatedly in the tail feathers by various female geese. The message was clear. There was no entrance into this tight-knit family for her. Each attempt that day and the next and the next was equally rejecting. Her lonely circling continued and her honking never stopped. It was loudest at night. I lost hours and days of sleep with her.

Last evening as the half-moon rose to clarify the night her honking wails began again, changing in depth of clarity as her body turned first east then west, south then north, searching for the response that would give meaning back to

Maggie Atwood
Newcastle, ME

her life. For hours the bereft honks rolled through the open slats of the blinds in my bedroom until around midnight I rose from my own fearful space, and in the moonlight I walked down through the field to the edge of the water. She saw me coming and watched me closely bobbing her head up and down between cries.

Slowly and with great care I greased my body from head to toe preparing myself for the long swim. I lowered myself into the water and took up position next to her. I watched her feet treading water as the incoming tide rushed at us, then closed tight my fingers pushing the water out of the way to stay close to her. She cried again turning her head to the side so her ear would fully hear what was not coming back. I opened my mouth to mimic her, letting out a noise, tentative and raucous. Her head bobbed up-down, up-down frantically.

"You know about this!" I imagined her saying.

"Yes, bird, I do..."

Full of wonder, I practiced my wails, for now at last that inside feeling of mine had a voice. I kept treading water next to her. This night, I decided, was going to be a very long one indeed.

At early dawn, when first light began outlining trees and the world was no longer an essay on gray, we paddled to the east, wailing, one after the other, circling, rushing forward, dropping back, paddling in place. Once again soundless movement began coming to life on earth and each of us watched some tiny speck moving on the horizon, wondering if it would blossom into someone we loved.

Julia Rice
Milwaukee, WI

Valentine to My Child

Do I own you,
or does my love for you
set you free?
Do I insist that you be me,
or can you be mine and yours at the same time?
Must I, because I love you, pay your way,
enabling your extravagances and wastes?
Or may I love you tough,
forcing you to be me in your own way,
but making you find your own way in the world
like a prodigal child?
Have I succeeded in building myself within you?
Have you become your own mother?
Does your face in the mirror look like me
or look like you
or look like a new being that is part you
and part me and part itself?
Have we created a new life that is as far
from a clone as possible,
as new as a fresh-opened flower,
with the bulldozer's power
and the mountain's beauty?
Do I own you,
or does my love for you
set you free?

Peggy Trojan
Brule, WI

Zoo

We live in a cage
of our making
while round and round us
go the menagerie of natives
at their leisurely pace.
We look out, following
from window to window.
Common deer, crow or eagle,
coyote, bear, rabbit,
rare blue heron or fisher.
We watch them stroll
on their quiet carousel.
Now and then they freeze,
return our stare,
ears twitching, eyes unblinking,
assessing the danger
if we got loose.

Jim Andersen
Hermon, ME

Moose Tracks

Every time I see a moose along the edge of a back road, I remember the summer I was ten. My name is Andy Wilson. I grew up living beside a dirt road, fifteen miles northeast of Greenville, Maine on the lower end of Moosehead Lake. My world was big woods and wilderness.

My father used to say, "The trout will bite when the leaves on the alders are as big as a mouse's ear." So the time was right to fish. One of my favorite meals was pan fried trout and my mother's fresh baked biscuits.

The summer started with a fishing trip two miles up the stream that ran behind my house. My younger brother, Mikey, had to tag along of course or my mom wouldn't let me go.

"Andrew, watch out for your brother and stay close to the stream," she said, "so you won't get lost."

"I've been going up the stream to the beaver dam for as long as I can remember," I answered. "I won't get lost in these woods."

We grabbed our fishing poles and a can of worms, and headed up the trail. It was warm for this early in the year and we hadn't gone the first mile before Mikey was complaining about almost anything he could think of.

"Slow down, Andy. You're walking too fast," he yelled from around the bend of the trail behind me. "Mom said you've got to watch out for me and you can't see me if you're that far ahead."

"Come along then and at least try to keep up." I slowed down to let him catch up.

He managed to keep up with this slower pace, until I heard a thump and turned to see him lying on the ground. "What now," I asked

"I tripped on a root," he cried. As he picked himself up he

Jim Andersen
Hermon, ME

asked, "Why can't we fish in this part of the stream?"

"I've told you before, the fishing is better in the dead-water above the beaver dam."

"If it's dead, then how can there be fish there?" he asked.

"The water isn't dead," I explained. "It just means that it's not moving."

We fished until noon and I had four trout hanging on a stick that I cut to use as a fish stringer. Mikey managed to catch a log, a rock and a tree overhead. I stopped each time to get his hook unstuck.

I also listened to a constant whine of, "It's too hot. The black flies are biting me." And finally, "I'm hungry." So we sat on a log and ate the peanut butter and jam sandwiches and drank the Kool Aid that Mom had put in my backpack.

Above the beaver dam, the woods opened into a big meadow with mud holes scattered along both sides of the stream. Mikey yelled from behind me, "Help!"

He had stuck his leg in a mud hole and sunk up to his knee. I helped pull him out and told him, "You have to watch out. Some of these mud holes are so deep you'll go in over your head. You might end up in China."

As I pulled him out, his sneaker came off and I had to get a stick to fish it out. After I rinsed the mud out of it, Mikey put it back on. He limped along behind me with a squishing noise at every-other step.

As I fished the next spot in the stream, Mikey got bored and wandered off. It wasn't long before I heard him hollering again.

"Help! Help! Help!" This time he sounded frantic.

I hurried to his aid expecting to find him up to his waste in a mud hole.

"Look!" yelled Mikey pointing. He had discovered a baby moose in the middle of a big mud hole, stuck almost up to his head. The moose calf was lying still with his eyes closed.

I noticed big moose tracks all around the area. Some

Jim Andersen
Hermon, ME

were deep into the mud where the mother moose had tried to get to her baby. I took a quick look around to be sure she wasn't standing nearby waiting to charge at us.

We sat on the bank wondering what we should do. We thought the moose was dead, but then it opened its eyes.

I immediately jumped into action. I took out my fishing knife, went to the nearest fir tree and started cutting branches. I spread the branches on the mud so I could crawl out to the moose.

The calf looked scared and started to struggle, but this only caused it to sink deeper. I tried to pull it out but it was stuck.

"Come help!" I yelled to Mikey.

The two of us were able to free the moose. We all lay in a big mud-splattered pile. The moose calf didn't have enough strength to stand.

After washing us off in the stream, I noticed that the calf had an odd ear. His left ear was regular moose size, but his right ear was only half as big as normal.

I made a decision and told Mikey, "You carry my pack and the fish. I'll carry the moose."

"We can't take the moose home. Mom will get mad," said Mikey.

"We can't just leave it here," I answered. "It will die."

"But what about its mother?" he asked.

"She's not around," I said. "Come on it's getting late."

It was almost dark by the time we got home. It was a hard trip carrying even a baby moose down the trail along the stream. Mikey had complained the whole way about having to carry all of my gear. "You should try carrying a moose," I said.

Mom met us at the door and we told her our story. To our surprise, she didn't seem mad. She took one look at the calf and hurried into the house. She came out with a bottle of milk that she had attached a rubber glove to and then put a

Jim Andersen
Hermon, ME

small hole in one of the fingers. The moose immediately started drinking.

"He can't be more than two weeks old," said Mom. "And look at his funny ear."

When my dad, who was a woodcutter, got home after dark, they both agreed that the moose would have to go back in the morning. We pleaded to keep it, but Mom and Dad would not give in.

The next morning Mikey and I reluctantly started back up the trail with the baby moose, Wilbur, that's what we called him, on a leash behind us. I was not going to carry him back up to the beaver dam. Wilbur walked along slowly on his spindly legs.

It was almost noon by the time we got back to the mud hole. I checked to see if there were any signs that the mother moose had come back, but there weren't any fresh tracks.

Mikey and I sat on a log and ate our lunch. Wilbur ate half of my sandwich. He liked the strawberry jam.

We made him lie down in the open grass along the stream to wait for his mom to return. We walked a little into the woods and watched from behind a tree to make sure Wilbur didn't follow us. Then we headed for home.

I heard Mikey sniffling behind me. "Come on, Mikey. Keep up." I didn't want to turn around because I had tears in my eyes too.

An hour after we got home, Mikey yelled, "Look!" and pointed to where the trail came out of the woods. There was a small fir tree on the edge of the clearing with a moose's head sticking out of the branches. It was Wilbur.

Dad said, "The mother must not be around, so I guess it wouldn't hurt to keep the calf around until he's old enough to take care of himself."

"He can't come in the house," said Mom. "You will have to make a shelter for him. Andy, you and Mikey are responsible for him. So keep him out of trouble." I wondered what

Jim Andersen
Hermon, ME

kind of trouble a moose could get into.

We spent the summer with a moose following us wherever we went. Wilbur went on our fishing trips. At first, he would jump into the middle of the stream and scare the fish, but as he grew he learned to wade into the slower water above the beaver dam and feed on the tender green plants that grew on the bottom.

Wilbur learned to play hide-and-seek with us and would stand behind a small fir tree. As the summer passed he grew so rapidly that when he hid behind the same tree, his head would be out of sight, but the rest of his body would still show.

Word got around about our moose with one small ear. Out-of-state fishermen would stop and take pictures of the moose in our yard. Sally Stevens, a girl that I went to school with, would walk two miles from her house to feed apples to Wilbur.

"She just comes to see you," Mikey teased.

Wilbur grew rapidly because he would eat almost anything. I found out what kind of trouble a moose could be. He ate the flowers in Mom's window boxes. He also ate half a bag of potatoes that was stored in the shed. Mom was not happy.

Then one day in the late summer Wilbur went too far. He was at an awkward stage with his big body supported by long, lanky legs. He broke through the fence that Mikey and I had put up to keep him out of the garden. He ate some of the vegetables and trampled most of the rest.

This time Mom was mad. "He has grown too big. He has to go. That's final."

That afternoon Dad loaded Wilbur into the back of his truck. "No, you can't go with me," he told us.

Mikey ran into the house crying as I stood and watched Dad's truck disappear up the dirt road into the woods. Just before it was out of sight, Wilbur turned as if to say good-bye. I'll never forget his funny-looking moose head with its one

Jim Andersen
Hermon, ME

normal ear and one small ear.

Two years later in the early summer, Mikey and I headed for the fishing hole. Mikey was older now and was leading the way. He had become a pretty good fisherman.

Mikey stopped so suddenly that I almost ran into him. I realized that we had walked into a dangerous situation. A bear cub was getting a drink at the stream and we had walked between it and its mother.

"Hold still Mikey. Don't move," I whispered, hoping not to excite the bear.

The mother bear growled and started toward us to protect her cub.

There was a sudden braking of branches and a very large bull moose stepped onto the trail between the mother bear and us. He lowered his big set of antlers toward the bear, pawed at the ground and grunted.

The mother bear made a soft growl and the cub crossed the trail to join her. They turned and disappeared into the woods.

As the Bull Moose started to walk away he turned and to our surprise we noticed he had one small ear.

Andrei Lougovtsov
Yarmouth, ME

Death by Music

The midday Portland sun beat down on my back as I walked towards my doom. At the time, my destination really did seem like instant death, using the alias of "Piano Recital" to mask its true, perilous persona. Its partner, going by the name of Anxiety, was tagging along with menace. It had already poisoned me down to my bones, quivering in their tendons and ligaments with fear. There must have been a toxin hidden in this simple term for a musical presentation, for I was slowly being tortured by the flames sparked with these locutions. If I slipped up on just one small, seemingly unimportant note and had to restart a section, this whole performance would not be a simple recital. It would be a death by music.

"Andrei, relax. All you do is play for a couple of minutes," encouraged Alex, my older brother. These words had absolutely no positive effect on me. I couldn't help thinking about the fact that he had never done anything like this before; he didn't know the feeling of imminent annihilation that traveled with these kinds of shows. I didn't want to talk; I just wanted to have time to think without being rudely interrupted by an object outside of my brain. This generally meant everyone and everything in my vicinity.

My family and I walked another block in silence. A lone cloud lingered in the sky above us. The air coming in from Back Cove smelled delicious, and I savored its flavor for as long as I could, for after I entered the performance building, I would get no more fresh air for as long as two or three hours. We were walking only about a hundred meters away from the source of the fragrant breeze, which was somehow making it seem even hotter outside. If there were no buildings or roads surrounding us, we would be in a natural paradise; birds chirping and flowerbeds threatening to overtake

Andrei Lougovtsov
Yarmouth, ME

freshly mowed lawns. Of course, no houses would probably mean no perfectly trimmed flowers either, but paradise here was still a delightful idea.

Alex decided to interrupt my daydream. "Well, here we are. Starbird Piano and Organ Gallery. This is where we're going, right?" My brother tilted his head to look at the white sign with the words "Starbird Music" imprinted in a black, almost gothic, font. It may have not been meant to scare children, but it certainly intimidated the nine year-old positioned in front of its canvas canopy.

I stepped forward and opened the door, holding it open until everybody was inside. A clump of golden bells gently rang upon movement, the sound resonating through the small building. And what a building it was! Pianos of all kinds, tall and short, skinny and fat, were scattered around the building. Some were painted a glossy black, while some shone in a deep mahogany. Electric pianos were housed in a minuscule corner of the shop, while multicolored music books were lined up facing the counter. This created a perfect aisle for me to walk through, as though I were going to receive a prize in a crowded auditorium. That pathway was leading right towards the room where the recital would be held, a convenient lane straight to my fear: the piano recital.

"This is where we bought your piano, Andrei!" exclaimed my mother. In fact, my piano was a good electric keyboard, not a cheap one like you might see in a school music class, but one of the full-bodied, non-fragile instruments. Still, it was no match for the booming grand piano that my teacher owned: a beautiful (and quite rare) Yamaha C-3.

I ignored her and continued on my death march towards the door of fate. It was difficult to believe that, only nine months ago, I had clambered onto the teacher's giant piano stool for the first time. At that point in time, I still had had my brother's old electric keyboard, a tiny and unworthy piece of scrap in my opinion. It was hard to imagine playing on it now, seeing as I was so used to proper instruments.

Andrei Lougovtsov
Yarmouth, ME

I somehow found myself standing before a gargantuan wooden door looming above me, serving as a monument to all fears in this world. Its golden handle gleamed in the sunlight streaming through the windows. The placid rectangle stared at me, as though it had an evil plot in mind; quite similar as to when somebody gives you a compliment with a flame in their eyes, in fact. It smiled at me, ivory teeth fully exposed in a gesture of welcoming. Yet even this could not disguise its purpose. That door was meant to guard one of my worst nightmares: a performance in front of a silent, attentive crowd.

My thoughts were shattered when the door suddenly creaked open, a result of my mother stepping in front of me, grasping the bright yellow bulb sitting on the right side of the anxiety-inducing plank, twisting it, and yanking it towards herself.

"Well, what are you waiting for? Go in!" cried my brother in a very harsh tone.

"Yes, Andrei. Keep moving," agreed my father in a much calmer voice than my dear sibling standing beside me. They must not have understood my panic at that point, because they were becoming impatient. I knew what I had to do. Stepping forward ever so cautiously, I ventured forth into the unknown.

The result of this petite journey was a short hallway, covered with blue and white tiles. The right side of the corridor housed a very long mirror, and bathrooms rested on its left. I could see the performance room straight ahead. As I walked further down the passageway, I began to see chairs everywhere in the auditorium, as well as a stage with a fairly oversized piano sitting atop it. My parents thought the instrument was beautiful; I thought it looked quite fat.

Upon entering the actual room, I noticed it was empty except for my piano teacher, sitting on a small black chair. Two tables were lined up next to each other, covered with a light beige tablecloth. A basket filled with programs sat in the

Andrei Lougovtsov
Yarmouth, ME

middle of the conjoined tables, almost begging us to take a leaflet and read it from cover to cover.

"Why, hello there!" exclaimed my piano teacher, her mocha-colored face lit up with joy. "Take a program, Andrei, and go practice for a few minutes on the piano."

I nodded, grabbing a few programs and handing them to my parents. Then I ambled up to the stage and sat myself down on the ebony leather piano stool. It was perfect for my height, not too high nor too low. The dim lights seemed to be taunting me, a constant reminder that this was just practice. The real performance would be far more treacherous. If those lights had been alive, I'm sure they would have found the idea of a nine year-old boy playing in front of such a seemingly strict, formidable audience quite humorous, as though the boy would have a complete memory lapse in the middle of a piece and walk off the stage in a flood of tears. I was determined not to let this happen.

I positioned my small, tender hands on the pearl-white keys of the piano, letting them hover there for about five seconds. The entire room faded into a blur; it had shifted out of focus. All that was visible was the great piano, towering above the small chairs. A tyrant in a hero's clothing.

Taking a deep breath, I hesitantly struck the first few notes of my lively sonatina. The keys succumbed to my press easily; they were just a tad harder to push down than a hot knife through butter. The sound they made echoed into the hallway and back into the deep bowels of the piano. There it lingered for a few seconds, the heavy timbre vibrating inside of the palatial instrument. Then I truly began to play.

The notes were springs under my fingers, light and jumpy. The sharp staccatos pierced the magnificent midnight luster of the instrument, detached notes hopping up and down. Afterwards came the smooth legato, the left hand providing support for the right. They all met during the finale, in which every thought put into the piece suddenly collided with a brilliant explosion of color and beautiful

Andrei Lougovtsov
Yarmouth, ME

sound. The mellow clapping of the still-small audience seemed distant; I was intoxicated by the inflection of the music as I clambered down from the stage and slumped down into my chair, feeling exhausted but satisfied. I had not noticed that a few families had crept into the room during my practice time, taking seats wherever they pleased in the auditorium. Right there and then was when I learned that playing an instrument can be just as tiring as a physical sport. In some regard, it could have been a form of athletics, with competitions and play-offs around every corner. Everything depended on your point of view.

"Very nice work," commented my father from beside me, a wide grin spreading across his face. "Now just play like that in the real performance."

I nodded, acknowledging him. No meaning was put into this shake of the head, as I seemed to have gone into a coma. The world went by in a swirl of color, children and adults walking up to the stage to rehearse while more visitors poured into the room. It became quite stuffy and hot and uncomfortable, not to mention the fact that nearly every person in this little cabinet held a video camera to tape every single event of the performance.

I didn't notice the time that had gone by. Before I knew it, I was forced to go back up on the infernal stage. But now it was different. This was going to be the real thing; absolutely everyone that was packed into the auditorium would be listening. Any mistake would supposedly be catastrophic. The euphoria of the rehearsal had passed; I was now scared out of my wits. As a result of my "coma," I missed every music piece played by the previous students. The only way I knew it was my turn was because my father nudged me with his elbow with his free hand. Of course, his free paw was gripping a video camera. All the more reason for me to be stressed.

"Andrei, it's time for you to play!" my dad whispered into my ear as everyone was clapping for the performer before me.

Andrei Lougovtsov
Yarmouth, ME

Seeing as I had already been shaken out of my stupor, I found no good reason not to go up and play again, although I'm sure I would have protested if I'd had even the slightest choice in the matter. Unfortunately enough, I didn't.

I clambered up onto the stage once more and took a short bow. My reply was a fairly loud clap from the viewers. I thought that my heart would beat out of my chest and spray red liquid over the people now watching me, their eyes seeming to bore holes into my suit. This fear was combated with a message from my brain, which decided to tell me to sit down on the piano stool and play. Seeing as there was nothing I could do to fight this dispatch, I moved my way over to the bench, took a deep breath, and laid my hands over the keys. The dim lights cast a rufous glow around the room; they apparently had taken to taunting me once more, sticking their tongues out at me and laughing. Of course, this did not really happen, but my mind read the information it was receiving from the eyes in this way.

Despite this horrible bullying by the lamps, I composed myself and began to play. Once again, a feeling of bliss washed over me the second my fingers pressed the ivory boards, and once again I felt the need to succumb to it. The music flowed like water under my fingers, smooth and silky with a touch of what could be classified as masterpiece. It was a pity that I did not have a longer piece to play, for the music seemed to have ended just as quickly and suddenly as it had begun.

I let the final chord sink into the piano and vibrate its insides, then took my hands off the planks and paused for a few seconds before rising from my seat and taking a short bow. Applause ricocheted off the walls and into my ears, creating a miniature earthquake inside my head. I walked off the stage to the remaining claps, much quieter and softer than the ones I had heard just seconds ago. As I sunk back into the firm sable chair once more, I barely heard my father whisper, "I loved your playing, Andrei. You hit every note

Andrei Lougovtsov
Yarmouth, ME

with no mistake!"

As usual, I gave an ambiguous nod, my eyes staring off into some faraway land beyond the reaches of anyone outside of my mind. I was, in fact, listening to the music the other musicians played, and simply did not want to be bothered by any petty outside causes.

My attentiveness was shattered by a female voice. "Wow! I'm so proud of you, Andrei. That was amazing!" my mother murmured into my ear.

"I do try to succeed, you know!" I replied, grinning from ear to ear. I said it in a final sort of tone, one that proclaimed my current target: relaxation. Mother got the hint, and with a final smile, turned back around and watched the remaining pianists make their way through their repertoires of varying difficulty. I slouched back and let the music wash over me like a cool fog on a hot summer day. My dream session ended abruptly when my piano teacher walked up onto the stage with her cane and signaled the end of the recital with a speech.

"Well, what can I say? I've had a wonderful year with all of you, no matter how much yelling and screaming has come out of it," A round of laughter carried across the room at this sentence. "I truly hope to see you all in a week or two for routine lessons. My only request now is for a quick group picture!"

She gestured for all of her students to join her on the stage. We brought flowers of many different kinds and presented them to her. Of course, she thanked each and every one of us before huddling us together for a photograph. Everyone was smiling, not necessarily for the picture, but because they had enjoyed a successful performance, and were quite obviously in high spirits.

"Everybody smile!" said a handful of parents with their cameras in position for a wonderful image. A second later, there were about 20 flashes across the room, and then a loud cheering. We poured off of the stage and into the crowd, not

Andrei Lougovtsov
Yarmouth, ME

forgetting to thank the teacher for her hard work.

"Are you ready to go?" asked my brother.

I smiled and replied, "Yes, Alex. Of course I am." With that, I turned and walked towards the door, linking hands with all my family and pulling them close to me. I couldn't stop a grin from creeping onto my face, for I had conquered my fear: my fear of the public performance. It would still come back annually to haunt me before my once-a-year recital, but for now, the anxiety was gone. I now understood. There was no such thing as death by music; there was only happiness.

***

George Wentz
Sturgeon Bay, WI

Mort's Requiem

Isn't Autumn a fitting time for death;
when vitality and energy are spent
and love's no longer in the air --
before cold wind comes on winter's breath?

Now reflect upon our paths of life
that brought us to this place
where, in devout silence,
there is peace instead of strife.

I raise a glass of wine in solemn toast
before this final feast of Cassoulet:
To you, Mort Canard, dear friend
for giving more than most.

Emily Lewis
Liberty, ME

The Gray Lady

Adrian Maddox clumsily unfolded the nearest newspaper in the deserted compartment and smirked as his narrow brown eyes found the obituaries. They darted eagerly over the untold stories, the brown of spring's mud pooling in his irises as his churning stomach boyishly reveled in an unspoken forbidden pastime.

Hmm, Faye Daven, he thought, his eyes settling on the name of one of the newly dead. *She could have a story...*

His mind roiled with curious musings as the hairs on the back of his neck brushed irritatedly against his coat collar and his eyes met the intrigued gray ones across from him.

He started, carefully peering at the soft figure pretending to bend over her book, dark hair curtained across her cheek. He saw her blushing shyly at him behind his newspaper, and a warm feeling rose from his stomach and met his smile with a quiet "Hi."

"Hi."

The train clattered gently, a companion in their midnight wanderings.

His mind sped through limited topics of conversation, resting finally on the least creepy.

"Um," he said intelligently. "Where are you off to?" Nope, still creepy. He bit his lip.

"Not sure yet," she said with a soft smile. "I like coming on at nighttime. It's quiet."

"Yeah." He wished he had such an idyllic reason for clambering onto the train in the hours designated "nighttime" that lurked like a black hole in the morning before reasonable waking time.

She turned back to her book as another rose of a blush spread slowly across her pale cheek. The purring heater, remarkably necessary for an October night, turned off

Emily Lewis
Liberty, ME

abruptly and the hollow silence was filled thickly with its absence and their furtive glances at each other, like peanut butter oozing creamily between two cookies.

She turned to him finally. "Do you come on often this late?"

He exhaled quietly, relieved she hadn't asked the obvious question. He rubbed the conspicuous bandage instinctively. "No, I got held up tonight." He gestured to the suitcase next to him.

"What do you do?"

"I'm an actuary."

"Boring." She crinkled her tiny nose and smiled without her teeth, meeting his gaze again. Her eyes set an inferno down his spine that made it crumble and fall like a magnificent, towering structure collapsing into the dust.

"What about you?" he asked, his voice trembling slightly. He wasn't sure that he'd ever met someone as lovely as her.

"I used to review books." She fingered the page corner she'd dog-eared.

"Oh." The silence clung to his skin and he unconsciously rubbed his hands together to brush it off. "What are you reading?"

"*Gatsby.*"

Adrian nodded, hoping to appear as though he'd read it. "What do you think?"

"Oh, I've read it a fair few times before," she said, avoiding his question with a tinkling laugh punctuated by another of those quiet smiles. His heart melted.

"So," she said suddenly. "What happened to your nose?"

He blinked. The words scrambled up his throat, fighting at once for freedom, and clogged his voice. The clever response he'd planned was lost in his stifled throat, leaving him only with an incoherent squeak of "What?"

Her eyes lingered over the thick greying bandage wrapped across his nose as she mumbled an apology.

His mind wandered to that day—was it only last week?

Emily Lewis
Liberty, ME

Him sprinting from the office, convinced he was chasing a peculiar dog no one else had seen, and watching as though from another's eyes as his hand slipped on the handle of the front door and his feet simply kept going.

He smiled gently at her. "I ran into a door." He couldn't help but laugh slightly at the absurdity of it. He didn't mention the dog.

"Oh." She swallowed a giggle. "Sorry."

"Nah, it's understandable."

They settled into silent companionship, flicking occasional warm glances at each other from the safety of their seats. Adrian receded into his paper, his mind flitting across stories for the many lost. He glanced up and she was beside him. He jumped slightly.

"May I look on?" she asked shyly. "Even *Gatsby* can get boring after the sixtieth time."

He nodded and sheepishly turned the paper to a different page. Her head hovered inches above his rigid shoulder, her hair carefully pulled aside. She was cold beside him; he wanted to reach a hand over and clasp her shoulder, pulling her close to him. The train rattled reproachfully at him.

"Hey," he murmured. "Um, sometime would you want to go somewhere...?" He turned to glance at the figure beside him and met only a vacant seat. He leapt up, bewilderedly searching the empty compartment as the train nonchalantly clattered and checked the locked doors, wishing he'd asked her name... He caught sight of the worn book sitting mockingly on the opposite seat. In the front, scribbled in untidy blue pen, was *Faye*.

She was gone.

GOOSE RIVER ANTHOLOGY, 2014

We seek selections of fine poetry, essays, and short stories (3,000 words or less) for the 12th annual *Goose River Anthology, 2014*. The book will be beautifully produced with full color cover and hard covers will have a full color dust jacket.

You may submit even if you have been published before in a previous edition of the *Goose River Anthology*. We retain one-time publishing rights. All rights revert back to the author after publication. You may submit as many pieces as you like.

EARN CASH ROYALTIES. Author will receive a 10% royalty on all sales that he or she generates.

There is no purchase required and nothing is required of the author for publication. Deadline for submissions is March 31, 2014. Publication will be in the fall of 2014 (they make great Christmas gifts). Guidelines are as follows:

- Submit clean, typed copy by snail mail—**mandatory**
- E mail a Word or Word Perfect file to us (if possible)
- Reading fee: $1.00 per page
- Do not put two poems on the same page
- Essays and short stories should be double-spaced
- SASE for notification (.46 cents) plus additional postage for possible return of submission if desired
- Author's name & address at top of each page of paper copy and first page of e mailed copy.

Submit to:
Goose River Anthology, 2014
3400 Friendship Road
Waldoboro, ME 04572-6337
E mail: gooseriverpress@roadrunner.com
www.gooseriverpress.com